Clean Contemporary Romance

CHERRY TREE
Island

DAISY LANDISH

Abby

ABBY WALKED around the house that had been her home for the last twenty years. Without all their things, it really was just a house. One that would be the pride and joy of another family in a few minutes. She took out her phone, snapped a picture of Kim and Kyle's growth chart in the garage, and sent it to them, just in case. It was the only thing they couldn't bring with them.

It had been a hectic month of June. The kids had completed their final exams in the third week of June, quickly followed by prom, which had also doubled as the twins' eighteenth birthday party.

Abby had been decluttering, sorting, and packing for weeks, but the kids had been busy studying and swore they would have their stuff ready to ship by the end of the month. The new owners wanted to celebrate the Fourth of July in their new home, and Abby had agreed to a July 2nd handover.

The movers had arrived at seven am. Kyle and his friends had loaded his boxes and remaining furniture onto the moving truck heading to New Jersey. He would be staying with his dad while interning at a small theater production company for the summer. He would be starting film school in New York City in the fall.

"Make sure you text me regularly, so I know you're safe," said Abby, tearfully hugging her son tightly.

"I promise, Mom. You be sure to do the same. I don't like knowing you'll be alone on a deserted island for two weeks," he replied.

"I won't be alone. There's a caretaker. Her name is Roberta, aka Bobbi, and she's apparently ex-military. I'll be perfectly safe. And the island isn't deserted; it's a twenty-minute boat ride from Stonington. Furthermore, it's completely self-sustaining. It has a garden, solar power, and its own freshwater lake. Don't worry, Kyle. I'll have the time of my life!" said Abby.

She gave him another quick hug before waving him off. Kim was by her side, and they were both crying.

"I'm going to miss him," said Kim. Turning to her mother, she added, "But not as much I'll miss you."

Abby held her baby girl and stroked her hair. She had known this would be difficult for all of them. But Kim, as free-spirited as she was, always had a more challenging time separating from her family members. Other than the week the kids spent with their dad over the Holidays and the two weeks during the summer, they'd never been apart. But that was about to change.

Kim received a full scholarship for the Marine Biology program at the university in New Brunswick, Canada. It was only a few hours away from Maine, but with Abby not having a new home yet, Kim was still a little unsettled.

"Don't worry about Kim, Mrs. Morgan. I'll keep an eye on her this summer," said Beatrice, Kim's best friend, as she closed the sliding door to yet another moving van.

This one was heading to St. Andrews, where Kim and Beatrice would spend their fall term. The intensive 12-week immersion semester in a marine setting provided students with a "hands-on" study experience of diverse marine organisms, including whales, seals, algae, fish, and invertebrates.

Once there, the girls would be joining a group tour of the Maritime Provinces: New Brunswick, Nova Scotia, and Prince Edward Island. The six-week tour helped new students familiarize themselves with the coastal ecosystem present in Eastern Canada.

Abby hugged both girls and made them promise to drive safe and let her know that they had arrived safely.

"I love you, Mom," yelled Kim from the truck window as it pulled away.

"I love you, Kimmie," yelled back Abby, waving enthusiastically with one hand and wiping the tears with the other.

Abby went back inside and oversaw the loading of the remainder of their furniture onto the moving truck, heading to a local storage facility until Abby was ready to send for them.

Now that the movers had left and the cleaning crew had erased any remaining traces of their lives, Abby felt ready for the handover.

As though on cue, Abby heard a knock and a "Hello?" from the front hall. It was exactly noon, as agreed.

"Hello!" she replied and rushed to greet Marney and Simon, the new owners, and their three adorable children.

They had finalized all the details with the notary a week before. This was a symbolic handoff. Abby gave them the keys, a list of her favorite shops and restaurants in the neighborhood, and wished them good luck in their new home.

Next, Abby stopped in at the local library to have lunch with Marge, the Librarian. Abby had started volunteering a few hours per week when the kids had started school. After years away from the workplace, she hadn't been ready to juggle a career and raise a set of twins all by herself. Fortunately, the monthly child and spousal support she received from her ex were more than enough to cover their living expenses. Volunteering had seemed like an excellent way to get out of the house and give back to the community. Her schedule had been flexible, and she was able to work around the many outings and events she volunteered for at school as well. When the kids started high school, she'd increased her hours at the library.

Marge wasn't only her boss, she'd been a confidante over the years, and Abby would miss her. Marge had been her go-to person for child-drearing advice, with four kids of her own and seven grandkids. As Abby had no siblings and both her parents had died a year after getting married, Marge had been her very own fairy godmother.

"So, how do you feel?" asked Marge, digging into the poke bowl Abby had picked up at the local sushi shop.

"I thought I'd fall apart," replied Abby. "Sure, it was hard saying goodbye to the kids. But, honestly, leaving the house wasn't as bad as I thought it would be."

"You've been preparing for this for a while now. And, as it is for a lot of single parents, you've been working non-stop for years. You're due for a break," said the elderly lady.

"On that, we can agree. I mean, the kids pitched in a lot. But caring for them and that big house has been my full-time job, and, other than the weeks they spent with their dad, I never got any time to myself," said Abby.

"And it took you years to start enjoying those weeks when the kids were away. Do you remember how you cried that first time?" asked Marge, setting down her fork.

Abby nodded. She remembered crying her eyes out as Paul drove away with her babies that first time. Well, the twins were four, more toddlers than babies, but still. Marge had come over and stayed with her that first night, soothing her fears and reminding her that Paul was a good father and that her children would be safe. Abby had been so afraid he wouldn't bring them back. But a week later, they were back. They'd had a great time but were as happy to be reunited with their mom as she was to have them home safe.

She shivered and said, "Don't remind me; those were dark days. But with your help, it only got better from there. I'm going to miss you, Marge."

They had finished their lunch, and it was time for Marge to get back to work. Abby could have stayed in Bangor and eventually taken over for Marge when she retired next year. But she felt she was ready for something new. And so, with a promise to keep in touch, they hugged and said a tearful goodbye.

Abby got back into her car and headed for the coast. The closer she got, the more tension seemed to drain from her body. Abby was looking forward to this new chapter of her life. She'd fallen in love with the private island when her realtor had shown her the listing. Reluctant to make an offer sight unseen, when her own house was sold much faster

4

than anticipated, she was suddenly homeless. The realtor had suggested she rent the property for two weeks and see how she liked living on a self-sustaining island.

"If you're still in love with it, we'll use the fee as your deposit and take it from there," she'd said, and Abby had agreed it was a perfect plan.

When Abby crossed the Deer Isle Bridge, she started getting excited. What an adventure this was going to be! She'd always loved the coast, and the idea of owning her very own private island made her giddy. She loved everything about it. Though the main house only had one bedroom, there was a guest house called *The Annex*. When her kids visited, they could stay there and even bring their friends. She could just imagine spending Thanksgiving and summer holidays with them and later, with their spouses and children. *New life, here I come!*

Bobbi, the island's caretaker, would be waiting for her on the dock at three o'clock. Since the drive was only an hour and a half, she arrived with time to spare. Abby picked up some eggs, milk, and a few other items at the local grocery and followed the realtor's instructions to unload her things in front of slip number 205. She went to park her car in the spot reserved for her use and used the marina restroom. When she made her way back to the dock, she stopped and stared, slack-jawed, at the tower of muscles loading her worldly possessions into a boat.

Jake

WHEN THE REALTOR had written to Jake, saying she had a potential buyer for his private island, he couldn't believe his luck. Four months after putting it on the market, they'd hooked a fish. He knew a lot of people were interested in living off the grid. However, not everyone was ready to live off-grid on a five-acre island only accessible by boat.

Cherry Tree Island had been in Jake Carver's family for three generations. He remembered spending summers there with his grandparents. He'd spend hours quietly fishing with his father and grandad in the early mornings, and the rest of his time was spent roaming the island, chasing birds, and eating berries until he was sick.

An only child, he'd inherited the island after his folks had died in a car crash over fifteen years ago. At the time, he'd been too busy building his career at the most prominent hedge fund firm in Connecticut to deal with it. He'd hired a caretaker and made an appearance once or twice a year to do some fishing and see to the paperwork.

When Jake had turned forty, he'd moved to Portland to start his own firm. The three-hour trip to the island afforded him the perfect block of time to catch up on his reading via audiobooks. The fresh air and solitude helped clear his mind and readied him for the week ahead, and he started spending most of his weekends there.

After five years, his staff was fully autonomous, and he could let go of the reins. It was time to settle down and raise a family. For that to happen, he'd needed to start putting serious effort into dating. However, after a year of first and second dates, he started wondering if he should have looked for a wife while still in Connecticut. None of the women he dated in Portland seemed to want to get married and have kids. He was about to give up and move to the island permanently when he met Jennifer.

He'd met her at an open house she was hosting after moving to the Penthouse of his building. He hadn't planned on attending, despite receiving a personalized invitation. Who had a housewarming party and invited strangers? Though he hated large parties, or any party, really, he decided to attend, as it might be a good networking opportunity. Plus, he was curious to see the rooftop garden and pool the Penthouse boasted.

Though the Penthouse had lived up to the hype, it was Jen that took his breath away. She was tall, one of the rare women who could meet his eye without straining her neck. And those eyes! They were a catlike yellow made even more arresting against her Mediterranean complexion. Heiress to a shipping conglomerate, she had no career ambitions and said she couldn't wait to have kids.

They'd hit it off immediately, and within a couple of months, he'd proposed, sold his apartment, and moved in with her. They had so many social engagements that there was never any time to take her to the island. In the end, they'd agreed it wasn't the safest place to raise a family, and he put it on the market. When they came back from their honeymoon, they'd start shopping for a suitable home.

In retrospect, he wouldn't miss his bachelor pad. He wouldn't miss Jennifer either, for that matter, though he wasn't ready to think about the extent of her betrayal. He would have kicked himself if he'd let go of his family's heritage for a two-timing airhead. *The things we do for love,* he thought.

Though he wasn't thrilled about having a guest on the island for the next two weeks, he was grateful the realtor had suggested a rental instead of pushing for an offer, which he would have accepted in a heartbeat three weeks ago.

The last week had been hell. He'd been standing at the altar with Trent, his best man, in front of a church that was slowly filling with people when the wedding planner had moved out of the shadows. With her back to the crowd, she'd discreetly motioned with her head for them to follow her out into the hall. Jake, worried that something had happened to Jen, had joined her in three strides of his very long legs. When Trent joined them, she asked him to close the door of the rectory.

"Is everything okay with Jen?" he asked in a panic.

Instead of explaining, the wedding planner's face fell, and she produced a letter which she handed to Jake wordlessly. Jake stared at the envelope dumbly. He recognized Jen's handwriting. It was customary for future spouses to exchange gifts before the ceremony. Since they'd spent last night apart, he'd had his delivered to the Penthouse. It was a charm bracelet with a single charm attached, a pair of wedding rings. There was a second charm, a couple of baby booties in the box. The card had read '*Looking forward to starting a family with you.*' Maybe this was Jen's belated gift. He tore open the envelope in anticipation. Knowing Jen, it was probably tickets to a cruise or an African safari. Only it wasn't. It was a Dear John Letter.

"*Dear Jake,*

*I got your present last night, and it dawned on me that I am not ready to be a mother or even a wife. I know I said I was, and at thirty-two, you'd think I'd be chomping at the bit like all of my friends. But I'm not. I'm just not. There are so many things I want to do, so many places to see. I'm sorry I'm only figuring this out now. My timing sucks. But you have to agree that it would have been far worse if I'd come to this conclusion **after** we'd been married. You deserve a woman that's ready to give you a house full of babies, and that woman is not me. I hope you find her.*

Love, Jen"

The letter dropped to the floor, and he let out a soft "motherfucker." Alarmed, Trent bent to pick it up. "Go ahead and read it," said Jake.

The wedding planner had stepped away to give him some privacy. Jake called her back and asked, "Where is she?" through gritted teeth.

The woman was wringing her hands. "I'm so sorry, M. Carver. I don't know. I went out to greet her limo, but she wasn't inside. The driver gave me this letter and drove off," she said, her eyes filling with tears.

Trent took over. "Fiona, there isn't going to be a wedding. M. Carver is understandably upset and will need you to handle things from here on out. Don't worry, I'm sure M. Von Radley will be taking care of the bill, regardless," he said, putting his hands firmly on her shoulders. She swallowed audibly and nodded. "Yes, sir. Of course. I'll see to everything," she said as she smoothed down her dress, squared her shoulders, and raised her chin. "I'm a professional," she added, heading to the door of the church.

Trent grabbed Jake's arm and yanked him toward the side entrance. He had Jake wait inside while he got his car and drove it to the door. When Jake spotted him, he left the rectory and quickly got in the car.

The drive to the hotel was quiet. Jake had refused to go home with Trent. There was no way he was spending what should have been his wedding night with the cutest family ever. Trent's wife was on bedrest, days from giving birth to their fourth child. It was a reality that would hit too close to home. Trent dropped him off, checked him in, and promised to have his luggage sent over as soon as he could arrange it with the wedding planner.

Jake had spent the weekend brooding in his hotel room, watching violent action movies, and knocking back a six-pack every night. Since he had planned to be away from the office for the next six weeks while he was on his honeymoon, he couldn't distract himself with work. A bunch of well-meaning friends had reached out and invited him to stay with them, but Jake was in no mood for company. He couldn't face them after being so completely humiliated. Not only had Jen left him standing at the altar, but the tabloids had later reported that she'd been seen boarding her private jet with none other than Portuguese model Francisco Silva. He didn't turn the TV on again and stopped checking his social media accounts.

He called Trent to vent, but his buddy was at the hospital. Rosa had given birth to a healthy baby girl. Jake congratulated him and sent a fruit basket to the hospital with a stuffed monkey for baby Rosita.

On Monday, at his wit's end, he'd called the anonymous employee hotline he provided for his employees and ranted over the phone for a good hour and a half. He felt better and thanked the patient listener for her time. Per her suggestion, he stopped drinking, ate proper meals, and visited the hotel gym and spa daily. By Wednesday, he felt a little calmer and went to the Penthouse. He needed to clear his stuff from Jen's place before she came back. As he packed, he resisted the urge to take a seven-iron to her collection of porcelain dolls. Like the dolls, Jen had looked perfect on the outside but was hollow on the inside.

He stared at the bed they had shared and imagined his fiancé in some other bed with her new boy toy. It only rekindled the fire of his rage. There was no way he was going to spend the night there. He went back to the hotel to regroup and called a moving service to meet him there the next day. He pointed, and they packed. Everything was loaded into one of those storage cubes and delivered to a Deer Isle storage facility.

Friday, he played a round of golf with Trent and had dinner with the little family.

"What are you going to do now?" asked Rosa in her direct way. That was one of the things he liked about his best friend's wife. The tiny woman was fearless. She didn't beat around the bush.

"I'm going to be staying at the island until further notice. They're not expecting me back at work for another seven weeks," he replied.

"But what are you going to do about the tenant? Where will you stay? You're welcome to stay here until she's gone," said Trent.

"You guys are the best. But I need to work this out on my own. I called Bobbi and offered her two weeks of paid vacation. Bobbi's no fool; she agreed and hung up before I could change my mind," he said with a chuckle.

Both Trent and Rosa laughed. They had met Bobbi a few times when they'd stayed on the island with Jake.

"Either way, you're always welcome here, anytime," said Rosa as she hugged him goodbye.

"Thanks, guys. You're the best. When the baby is fit to travel, let me know, and I'd love to have you all over later this summer," he replied.

"We'll hold you to that. Drive safe, buddy," said Trent as he gave his friend a one-armed hug.

Jake hit the road on Saturday morning, leaving the whole mess behind him. He couldn't wait to chuck his phone, cast his rod, and catch some fish. The lake at the island was well stocked, and there was nothing like the early morning quiet of the lake to soothe what ailed you.

When he got to the marina, he found the tenant's things neatly stacked in front of his boat, but no tenant. Itching to get a move on, he started loading their stuff into the hold.

Abby

"I'm ASSUMING you're not Roberta," said Abby. Intent on his task, he appeared not to have heard her. She was about to repeat herself when the man turned, still holding her crate of fruits and vegetables, to scowl at her. Whatever he was about to say died on his lips as his gaze scanned her from head to foot. His features evened out, and he replied, "Bobbi's on vacation. I'm filling in."

Abby swallowed audibly. She stared, clutching her printed confirmation email, transfixed by the way he was efficiently stacking her crates and luggage with ease and precision. The cargo hold was large enough that he could have just dropped them in anywhere. No, this hunk of a man likely did nothing in half measures. Abby found this somewhat reassuring, and she relaxed a little.

He had to be at least six feet four inches, a good foot taller than her though she had yet to stand next to him. Clearly, he had things under control. To be on the safe side, she took out her phone to check in with Lucy, the realtor. Lucy wasn't aware of this last-minute change in caretakers and requested Abby discreetly take his picture. She'd only just sent it when her phone rang.

"That's not a caretaker. That's the owner!" said Lucy at the other end of the line.

"What?" exclaimed Abby, loud enough for the said owner to turn and look at her. She shrugged in apology while pointing at the phone. Turning, she quickly made her way down the dock for some privacy.

"What do you mean he's the owner? I thought you said he was in Europe for the summer!" she screamed into the phone in a panic. She was pacing on the dock, taking deep breaths. Abby didn't like surprises.

"He was! Hold on while I check my email and scroll the social media feeds," she replied.

Abby waited, keeping a wary eye on the man at the other end of the dock. He didn't look like a fancy businessman. Wearing well-worn jeans and a grey hoody with the Yale logo that had seen better days, he looked like he hadn't shaved in a few days. From the grey at his temples and in his beard, Abby put him in his mid-forties.

Lucy was back on the phone.

"He was supposed to have gotten married last week to some heiress, but I just read on the news feed that she stood him up and made off with an up-and-coming Portuguese model. He put the island up for sale when he moved into her Penthouse a few months ago," explained Lucy.

"That's horrible!" replied Abby, feeling for the hottie. She knew how it felt to be thrown over for a younger model. That might explain the scowl and the clenched jaw. "But why is he here, now?" she asked.

"I can only assume he's as hopeless as you are and had nowhere else to go," replied the realtor.

"Did he know I'd be here?" asked Abby, worried that Lucy hadn't consulted the owner before offering her the place for two weeks.

"I sent him an email three weeks ago to get his approval, and he was all for it. Said it was the perfect scheme to sell the place," said Lucy.

"But now he might not want to sell," whined Abby, as her stomach dropped. This couldn't be happening. Where would she live?

"If that's the case, then we'll look at some other options. For now, you've got a lovely waterfront home to stay in with your very own private beaches. Relax and enjoy it. You're overdue for a vacation. Besides, he'll be at the other end of the island in the caretaker's cabin. Close enough to lend a hand if things go awry, far enough that he won't be underfoot," soothed the realtor.

Abby bit her lip. She'd signed a contract and paid the fee. And she couldn't go home. "Okay. I'll call you if there's a problem," said Abby and hung up the phone. She took a deep breath, squared her shoulders, and walked back to the boat.

Jake

~∂∽∘

WHEN JAKE FINISHED LOADING the tenant's stuff alongside his own in the boat, he turned to tell her to get a move on. She was still talking on the phone at the other end of the dock. She was clearly upset, her ponytail swishing angrily every time she started pacing in a different direction.

She wasn't at all how he'd pictured her. He'd imagined a frumpy soccer mom come to mourn her empty nest in a seaside cottage. Abby Morgan was no soccer mom. She barely looked old enough to have kids, let alone grown children off to college. He hadn't been close enough to get a good look at her face, especially with those huge sunglasses women wore today. But her athletic build was evident in the short, form-fitting dress she was wearing. Not one of those frilly dresses Jennifer had him pick up from the cleaners. This was downright sporty but sexy as hell. Instead of strappy heels at the end of those shapely tan legs, he'd found no-nonsense slip-on canvas shoes. He'd muttered something about Bobbi instead of introducing himself like the gentleman his mother had raised.

She was heading back his way, and he made himself stop looking at those legs. This was someone's mother, and she didn't deserve to be ogled by the likes of him. He wiped his hands on his t-shirt, only now becoming aware that he hadn't shaved and was wearing his ugliest but most comfortable jeans. He'd been smart enough to hide these from Jen when she'd overhauled his closet.

"Miss Morgan, I'm Jake Carver," he said, extending his hand when she'd reached him.

"Pleased to meet you, M. Carver. My realtor has just informed me that you are the owner of Cherry Tree Island. I'm sorry to be putting you out of your own home," she said with an apologetic smile.

"Call me Jake. Don't worry about it. The caretaker's cabin is a lot nicer than it sounds. We should get a move on before the tide gets too low to leave," he replied in a low baritone.

"Alright, then. Call me Abby," she replied, accepting his hand to get into the small tugboat. He held out a life vest like it was a fancy coat, and she laughed as she fit her arms into it and hurriedly zipped it up before he got the notion of doing it for her.

"Do you want to sit in the cockpit or on the outdoor bench?" he asked. It was a gorgeous day, and she chose to sit outside to enjoy the view and the sea spray. He was surprised but didn't comment. He started the engine, and they were off.

Separated as they were, there was no conversation on the twenty-minute ride to the island. Abby enjoyed the ride though it was choppier than she had expected, and she kept a firm grip on the railing.

It reminded her of the summers she'd spent in Bar Harbour with her grandparents until they got too old to care for their summer cottage and sold it. She'd had such fond memories that she would drive from Bangor to Bar Harbour every summer with her kids and stay in one of the many seaside cottages. Aside from the usual beach activities, she and the kids had enjoyed hiking in Acadia National Park. This was the first summer they wouldn't be going there as a family, and she hadn't had the heart to go without them.

The boat was slowing. When the house came into view, she fell in love with it all over again.

"Give me a minute. I'll get the trailer to bring your things to the house," said Jake as he stopped the boat and tied it to the dock.

Abby

WHILE SHE WAITED, Abby started to bring her things up from the hold and onto the deck.

Jake backed up the trailer as close as he could and told her he could handle their stuff and she could walk on ahead to the house. But Abby wasn't having this poor man wait on her hand and foot.

"It'll be faster this way," she replied and kept ferrying the contents of the hold onto the dock. He shrugged and brought her things onto the trailer. With little to no conversation, they made quick work of it. They made a good team.

As there was only one seat in the tractor, Abby followed Jake up the path to the house on foot. It wasn't very far, and it gave her a chance to get her bearings.

Abby was used to doing things for herself. This wasn't an all-inclusive vacation, and though she'd been prepared to let Roberta give her a hand and show her the ropes around the property, this was an entirely different situation. The owner would likely not be selling and would see no need to explain how everything worked beyond what she would require for a two-week stay.

He'd clearly just been through an ordeal, and she didn't want him feeling responsible for her. She'd raised her kids on her own, and experience had taught her that relying on other people only led to disappointment.

The main house, situated on the southern tip of the island, was a two-story colonial home with a wraparound porch to take in the ocean views. It was even more gorgeous than in the pictures she'd seen online. She knew the main floor was a large open living room with cathedral ceilings, a massive fireplace, and a well-equipped kitchen. The master bedroom occupied the upper floor loft. Complete with its own ensuite bathroom and a private balcony, it also had corkscrew stairs that led to the "widow's walk" on the roof.

When Abby walked up to the front door, she saw that Jake had already started unloading her things. She grabbed her suitcase and laptop bag, dropped them inside near the door, and then went back to get the remaining supply crate. She'd been told to bring the usual household supplies like dish soap, toilet paper, and paper towels, and the food she would need for at least a week. Though Roberta went to Stonington every week for supplies, Abby didn't want to impose and had brought enough for her entire stay. It was standard practice when traveling with kids to pricey vacation destinations. Planning ahead not only saved money but also saved time and a whole lot of hassle.

She placed the crate on the kitchen counter with the other ones.

"I'll get the power and water going while you unpack your supplies," Jake said, giving her a quick tour of the kitchen.

She put the perishables in the fridge. It was empty but for a jar of pickles and a box of baking soda, and it was spotless. She was putting the fruit and vegetables in the drawers when the lights went on, and the fridge started humming.

She tried the faucet, and water came sputtering out, a little murky at first but quickly turning clean and clear. She put away the cleaning supplies and the rest of the food in the pantry. She was collapsing her crates when Jake came back into the kitchen.

"You should be all set. Let me show you where to store those while I give you the tour," he said, stacking the crates and leading the way to a small utility closet beside the first-floor bathroom. He showed her how to turn the power and water on and off, where he kept emergency supplies, and the washer and dryer location.

"I guess you know how to use those already," he said with a wink. Abby nodded but didn't comment about the loads of laundry she no longer had to tackle with an empty nest.

Next was an alcove by the dining area set up as a home office. He pointed to a sticky note that had the Wi-Fi password and explained about the satellite TV offering.

"I don't watch TV, but I do watch a little Netflix," she said, taking in the large screen TV, extensive DVD collection, and game console that her presence would be keeping Jake away from for the next two weeks.

"It can get humid and chilly in the evening, even in July, so don't hesitate to start a fire," he said and proceeded to show her how to do it. There was plenty of chopped wood, old newspapers, and fire starters.

He scanned the room and made a beeline for her suitcase. She almost had to run the length of the room to beat him to it. "I've got it," she said, a little out of breath when he offered to carry it upstairs.

He frowned but led the way up the stairs to a gorgeous bedroom. The king-size bed had a simple oak headboard with matching bedside tables placed in front of tall yet narrow windows facing the woods. Jake went to the bathroom, checked the lights and water, flushed the toilet, and came back out.

Setting her suitcase on the bench at the foot of the bed, Abby turned to face a set of double patio doors. The view took her breath away. She saw the dock where they'd arrived and the bay beyond it. They were too far away to see the mainland, but Abby could spy one or two neighboring islands. She smiled and unconsciously inhaled deeply, letting her shoulders drop on the exhale.

Instead of the salty air, her nose caught a distinct male scent. Jake was standing right next to her, admiring the same view. She could feel the heat coming off his body and identified the alluring aroma now that he was closer. It was clearly not aftershave. It was most likely his soap or deodorant. She closed her eyes and took another inhale. How long had it been since she'd been this close to a man? She'd forgotten how good they smelled. She needed to get away from him, fast, or she'd make a complete fool of herself.

"Isn't it beautiful?" he asked as he strode to the patio doors and slid one open.

He stepped out onto the balcony and braced himself on the railing. The view had just improved exponentially. Had Lucy said what he did for a living? He had the physique of a swimmer, with broad shoulders, and a narrow waist. Perhaps he'd been on the Yale rowing team. His loose-fitting jeans didn't conceal his muscular build. This was bad. Where had this guy been after her divorce? She would have gobbled him up in an instant. Heat flushed her cheeks, and she immediately felt remorseful for objectifying him. She shook herself and joined him at the railing.

"It's one of the most beautiful places I've ever seen," she said as she repeated her inhale and exhale. This time, she could smell the distinct coastal aroma that could only be found in northern Maine.

"Come on, it's even better upstairs," he said with a grin, grabbing her hand and pulling her along. Her hand tingled. His hand was soft, not the calloused hand of a worker. Abby was too surprised to do anything but follow him. When they got to the stairs, he dropped her hand, mumbling a barely audible "sorry." He motioned for her to go up first, and she immediately regretted wearing such a short dress. She went up quickly, hoping he wasn't getting an eyeful of her functional underwear.

She ultimately dropped the thought when her head cleared the stairs. The widow's walk surrounded a tiny room with a window on three sides and a door that led to the balcony that surrounded it. There was only room enough for an old rocker. She opened the door and walked out, grabbing the railing when she felt the strong winds.

"It's my favorite place to drink an early morning cup of coffee," said Jake, coming out from behind her. "From here, you can see the whole island." Jake pointed to the guest house in the east. The Annex housed three additional bedrooms. It had no kitchen, nor was there electricity or running water. Seasonal guests could either use the facilities at the main house or make use of the outhouse and outdoor shower.

Next to a sizable garden, there was a greenhouse and a large shed. Beyond these, there was the swimming hole that the listing had mentioned. Abby thought it looked like a good lake; the water was clean and clear. It even had a little dock with a ladder, a chair, and a couple of kayaks.

Jake pointed to a patch of forest at the other end of the island. "That's where the caretaker's cabin is. You see the path there, the one that goes around the lake?" he said, leaning closer to Abby. He was making her nervous, but she nodded. "That leads to the cabin. All paths lead to the lake. The ones on either side lead to sandy beaches," he added. He placed a hand at the small of her back and led her to the front of the house. Again, she was surprised by this invasion of her personal space. It wasn't an inappropriate gesture, and his hand fell away when they'd reached their destination. It had lasted a few seconds at the most, and it had felt good. So good that Abby realized she'd been starved for physical contact of the male variety.

"That path goes around the island," he said. He gave her another once over and added, "You look like you might be a runner. It's about two and a half miles."

"I don't run, but I walk a lot, so I'll definitely check it out," replied Abby, wondering if the hottie was checking her out. Surely a guy as handsome as this, who dated thirtysomething heiresses, couldn't be into her. She gave an involuntary smile, then made herself wipe it off. This was how you got into trouble—lusting after men who would only break your heart.

"I should get my stuff to the caretaker's cabin and get settled before dinner," he said. She nodded and followed him down to the bedroom, then to the first floor. He fished into his back pocket and produced a card.

"This is my cell phone number if you need anything. Do you have any questions before I go?" he said as she took the card and saw he was a hedge fund manager from Portland.

"None that I can think of for the moment. Thanks for the tour. You've got an amazing property here," she said, extending her arms to encompass the room.

"Thanks. Enjoy your vacation," he said as he left and closed the door behind him.

She watched him get back on the tractor, drive down the path near the lake and disappear into the woods. Abby was torn between feeling anxious about her future and excited spend the next two weeks on an island with a hot guy.

Jake

〜⚭〜

JAKE GOT BACK on the tractor and headed for the caretaker's cabin. Bobbi had left both the power and water on, so he put his food away and placed his clothes away in a drawer she had emptied out for him. She had also left him a stack of clean sheets and towels.

He pulled down the murphy bed and put the sheets on the mattress, topping them with the standard-issue army blanket. Jake smiled to himself. *You can take the gal out of the army, but you can't take the military out of the old gal.*

The cabin was neat and simple, much like its usual occupant. Roberta was another one of his favorite people. The woman didn't have a single nonsense bone in her body. She was hardworking, never complained, and knew how to make herself invisible.

She was an excellent caretaker, handling all the required jobs with efficiency. She kept tabs on how much firewood they chopped, making sure to replace the trees they took down. She took care of the garden, the lawn, and most of the repairs around the island. Whatever she couldn't do herself, she'd outsource to a local on the mainland.

When Jake brought the tractor back to the shed, he saw everything was tidy in there too. Bobbi had left him a note and list of chores to do, should he feel so inclined. Otherwise, she'd get to them when she came back.

Jake was more than happy with the work. The manual labor helped him work through his feelings about being dumped at the altar. After a couple of days of chopping wood, mowing the lawn, and weeding the garden, he realized he wasn't heartbroken over losing Jennifer.

She was right; better to find out before the wedding. It wasn't even about the wasted time. All in all, he'd spent less than a year with her. *That should have been his first clue.* Mostly, his ego was bruised from the public humiliation. Trent was right when he said most people would move on and forget about it. The ones closest to him would likely blame Jen for the whole fiasco. No one was judging him for her actions.

He still felt he could have handled things better. If he hadn't been in such a rush to start a family, he would have paid more attention to the signs, and taken time to get to know Jen a little better. That was the rub. By jumping the gun, he'd set himself back a year in his quest for a wife and kids. He knew it ultimately didn't matter. Men didn't have age limitations for having kids, but he couldn't help the pangs of envy he got every time he was at Trent's house. He knew that the couple fought like everyone else and that their kids were mini hellions most of the time. Still, from his point of view, they had it all: a comfortable home, a loving partnership, and a brood of cubs.

He'd gotten a lot done since arriving on the island. The cabin didn't have Wi-Fi, and the solar panel was only strong enough to power the essentials. Thus, he'd gone through most of Roberta's books, for which he was glad was an endless supply of action-packed crime and detective novels. He hadn't had a beer all week, and the fresh air and daily exercise were doing wonders for his mood.

Had he been in the big house, he'd have been tempted to sit and watch TV or, worse, get some work done. As it was, he hadn't checked his email or social media accounts all week. He decided to take technology breaks more often.

This may have been Abby's vacation, but Jake was enjoying the R&R.

Abby

THE FIRST WEEK went by much too fast, but Abby stopped feeling bad for stealing Jake's home. If two weeks were all she was going to get in this little piece of paradise, she was going to enjoy them to the max.

She and Jake had settled into daily routines that never intersected directly, though Abby was acutely aware of her landlord.

Every morning, Abby woke early, made coffee, and went to enjoy it on the widow's walk, where she could watch the sunrise. That wasn't her only motivation. On her first morning, she spied Jake running along the trail. He did three passes, ending his run at the lake, where he stripped down to his boxers, jumped into the lake, and swam laps for about fifteen minutes.

Once, he spotted her on his way out and gave a quick wave. She waved back. As usual, he stretched out on the small dock to soak up the sun until he was dry enough to put his clothes and shoes back on and run back to his cabin.

The man was fit and as enjoyable to watch as the sunrise. Mother Nature hadn't gone wrong when she created him. Abby caught sight of the grey creeping into the curly hairs on his chest, even from this far away. *Why did men improve with age?* It was an unfair reality.

Abby knew she looked good for her age. She didn't dye her hair, embracing the grey as it spread slowly through her auburn locks. And though she didn't use a ton of products, she had a daily skincare regimen that gave her a youthful glow. Mostly, the secret was eating well, drinking water, and getting enough sleep. Of course, running after a couple of kids had helped keep her fit over the years.

In recent years, she'd been doing more and more hiking on her own as other things drew her kids' interests. She'd tried joining groups, even single hiking groups, but she found most people were too chatty when all she wanted was to appreciate nature. That's why the private island had appealed to her. It had all her favorite things: the ocean, beaches, and trails with none of the extra people cluttering the view and the silence.

She had felt a pang at the missed opportunity but consoled herself that, for a couple of weeks at least, Jake wasn't going to get in her way. And his lovely form was an excellent addition to the view.

After breakfast, Abby walked the trails and made a note of the best spots for sunbathing. Had she been alone on the island, or even if Roberta had been around, she would have loved to sunbathe in the nude. As it was, she kept her bikini on and always wore a cover-up to and from the beaches.

She was happy that she had thought to bring her beach chair. She would sit and read on the eastern beach after her walk in the morning, then head over to the western beach after lunch to lounge, listen to music, and nap. She hadn't realized how tired she'd been from the mad dash of packing and moving over the last few weeks. The idleness of her days was doing her good.

On her way back to the house to prepare dinner, she would often catch Jake puttering in and around the shed, working in the garden, mowing the lawn, or, her favorite, chopping wood. She would often come home to find a basket of assorted vegetables on the porch. Once, there had even been a fish wrapped in newspaper.

Today, however, the basket was full of tomatoes. Too many to eat on her own, especially as they were huge and very ripe. She set them to stew on the stove, thinking of making spaghetti sauce and debated whether to invite Jake to dinner to thank him for the bounty. She might have canned the sauce at home and expressed her thanks to a helpful neighbor by dropping off a container with a note. But she didn't have the necessary equipment here for that, and she was grateful to the man for respecting her privacy thus far.

She was weighing the pros and cons of her idea when there came a knock at the door. *Speak of the devil.* She called out, "Come on in, I'm in the kitchen."

She heard the screen door clang and heard shuffling as Jake removed his boots. Abby was sad to see that he'd put his shirt back on as he entered the kitchen. She was browning beef in a skillet, and he came close to her so he wouldn't have to yell above the sound of the fan.

"Do you need me to make a supply run into town tomorrow?" he asked.

"Is it Friday already?" she asked incredulously.

"I'm afraid so," he said with a nod of the head. "Time flies when you're having fun!" he added, taking an appreciative whiff. The beef was done. She nudged him out of her way and drained the fat in a pot near the sink. She didn't think she should be pouring it down the drain here. Once she was done, she carried the pan and poured the contents into the stewed tomatoes, adding some fresh basil and oregano she'd found in the garden. She stirred the sauce and reduced the heat to let it simmer.

"No, I don't need anything. But thanks for offering," she replied as she turned off the fan, her voice sounding shrill without the background noise.

It was a good-sized kitchen, similar to the one she'd had at home, but it felt tiny with him occupying most of the space. She had to invite him to dinner now, she thought. He was staring at the stockpot like a man who hadn't eaten in days despite evidence to the contrary.

"Thanks for the veggies, but there were way too many tomatoes today! Would you care to join me for a spaghetti dinner?" she asked.

A huge grin appeared on his face. It was the first time she'd seen him genuinely smile, and it took her breath away. *Of course, he had to have perfect teeth.* Did this man have any flaws?

"I'd love to, thanks for inviting me. If you like, we could have dessert at my place. I made a berry cobbler. We could sit out on the deck; it's got a great view of the sunset," he said so earnestly that Abby was speechless. Seeing her mouth hanging open, he laughed and added, "Don't look so surprised! I'm a forty-five-year-old man living alone on an island. If I couldn't cook for myself, I'd die of starvation! Besides, there's a huge raspberry patch right near the cabin. I couldn't let them go to waste."

Abby found her tongue in time to say, "Yes, of course. You seem like a very competent man." His left eyebrow lifted at that, and she immediately followed up with, "Dinner should be ready in about an hour if you want to wash up and change."

He looked down at himself, then at her. She was still wearing her bikini and cover-up, making her feel self-conscious. Her hair was dirty and in braids, and she felt about twelve years old, fidgeting in the kitchen.

Mercifully, his gaze moved on to something he saw through the window and his brows knitted before making his way to the door. "I'll be back around six if that's okay with you," he said, and she nodded. "I hope you brought a slicker because it looks like we might get some rain. Hopefully, it'll fall overnight, and you'll be able to resume your sunbathing regimen tomorrow," he said on his way out.

She was happy he couldn't see her flushed cheeks as she made her way up the stairs to jump in the shower. Had he been spying on her while she sunbathed? Surely not, she thought. He may have chanced upon her while doing some chores. And, given her daily attire and her ever-increasing tan, sunbathing was a reasonable assumption.

She washed her hair and resisted the temptation to take pains with her appearance. This was not a date. It was a dinner between neighbors, nothing more. Anyhow, she hadn't brought anything that was the least bit dressy since she'd planned to spend two weeks alone on an almost deserted island.

Still, she brushed out her hair, put on one of her sporty dresses, and applied a touch of gloss to her lips. It was nothing she wouldn't do when having dinner with a girlfriend, she reminded herself.

Just because Jake Carver made her drool, that didn't mean he felt the same way. And even if he did, the only possible outcome was her being his rebound relationship. She was single for a reason: she had yet to meet a man she could count on to be faithful, loyal, and reliable. After her divorce, when the kids got older, she'd dated but had never found that ultimate combination in a man whom she also found attractive. For a while, she had an on-again-off-again relationship with a guy she'd met on one of those hiking outings. They had great chemistry and enjoyed many of the same activities, like hiking and going to the beach.

But they never had a real connection; there was no emotional intimacy. Though the relationship was convenient in many ways, she'd ultimately ended it because she knew they both deserved better. At least, she did. She had vowed to stay single and celibate until she found the total package.

When Jake appeared at her door an hour later, freshly shaven and wearing a pair of khakis with a polo shirt, her attraction to him was threatening that vow.

Jake

ON THE WALK back to the cabin, Jake congratulated himself on scoring a homecooked meal. Though he'd boasted about his cooking skills, the truth was that he only knew a handful of recipes and was often too lazy to make them. It was far easier to just grill a steak and toss a salad than to get the whole kitchen dirty for a single meal.

When the fish had failed, he hoped the basket of tomatoes would lead to this specific outcome. He remembered his mom would make spaghetti sauce every Sunday from canned tomatoes. But the best sauce always came from fresh tomatoes in the summer, like his grandma had made.

Abby reminded him of his mom. She, too, had been an efficient and capable woman, taking pride in her role as a mom and housewife. When he'd looked around for such a woman when he was ready to settle down and start a family, he'd found them hard to come by and had all but abandoned the plan until he'd met Jen.

By no stretch of the imagination could Jennifer Von Radley be considered a suitable homemaker, but she had shown him a gentler side of herself and claimed a desire to have kids. So, he'd proposed and lived to regret it.

He had expected to spend the next two weeks at the beck and call of a pampered soccer mom. But Abby hadn't once asked for help. In fact, her attitude right from the start had been a little standoffish, like she was used to doing things her way. The way her chin had jutted in defiance when she'd pounced on her luggage still had Jake in stitches. He'd been wise to keep his comments to himself.

It was hard not to compare Abby and Jen. They were so different. Where Abby was fiercely independent, Jen had been clingy and useless. It was probably the product of being an heiress; she was used to having others do things for her. Even the size of Abby's suitcase was laughable. That tiny bag couldn't have held Jen's makeup, let alone enough clothes for two weeks.

Jen had her strong points. She was always relaxed and happy. It was one of the first things that Jake had noticed and appreciated about her. Most of the women he encountered were stressed and wore haggard expressions. Abby was somewhere in the middle. Though she didn't look worried, she did seem guarded, especially when he was around. There was a story there, he was sure.

When he'd spied her reading on the eastern beach, she'd worn a sweet smile like whatever she was reading was making her very happy. Absurdly, he wanted to do something to make her aim one of those smiles at him.

After lunch today, he'd caught her on the west beach in her hot pink bikini. That was his favorite. She had about three or four different ones that she rotated, but the ones she wore in the afternoon were skimpier than the others. This one had a cheeky bottom, which was much sexier than the thongs Jen had worn. It only showed the bottom part of her well-tanned and very round behind when she lay on her front.

Though she had perfectly lovely cleavage, this was the sight he waited to see every day. Not that he was a Peeping Tom or anything. Imagine a grown man spying on his tenant. He wasn't that crass. It was only that he'd heard her singing along with her headphones and walked over to see. The woman couldn't carry a tune; it was adorable. However, his amusement had quickly turned to lust when he saw that she was shaking her butt to the beat of the music, her whole body swaying to what had to be dance music.

He'd quickly retreated to the trees and only gave her a cursory glance before throwing his pent-up energy into his afternoon chores. Where Jen was tall and willowy, Abby had curves. The kind a man could really get excited about.

He wasn't stupid enough to think anything was going to happen between them. No, this wasn't a date. Sure, he'd taken the time to shave and put on the only decent clothes he'd brought with him. But that's what a gentleman did when invited to dinner. He was only sorry he hadn't thought to pick some flowers, but that probably would have been too much anyway.

When he knocked on the door promptly at six, she called out to him to come in and soon joined him in the kitchen. She was wearing one of her maddeningly short dresses again, padding around his kitchen in her bare feet. To avoid running his hand along her tantalizing thighs, he went to the cabinet in the dining room to retrieve a bottle of wine and some of the fancier glasses.

"Did you want to eat inside or out?" he called to her.

Her head popped out of the kitchen, and she replied, "Inside since you said it might rain."

He took out two placemats and set down the wine glasses. Carrying the wine back to the kitchen, he took out two pasta bowls and placed them next to the stove. She was draining the pasta. He squeezed past her, placing his free hand on her shoulder as he excused himself. He could have gone around the kitchen island to get to the bottle opener, but he couldn't help himself. Her hands were full, and she couldn't move out of the way. He got a kick out of being so close to her, even momentarily. Her hair was loose, damp from the shower, and starting to curl. He caught a faint scent of grapefruit. It suited her, fresh and straightforward.

He opened the bottle of wine, grabbed the utensils, and returned to the dining room to finish setting the table. When he came back, he was hit with the tantalizing aroma of fresh garlic and the view of Abby's ample backside as she bent to retrieve the garlic bread that had been warming in the oven. She blew a stray curl out of her face as she closed the oven door with a swing of her hips and deposited the bread on the counter.

"Dinner's ready!" she exclaimed. Removing the oven mitts, she handed him one of the pasta bowls and motioned for him to help himself. He took the bowl but stood there watching her slice the bread, grab a basket from above the fridge like she'd done it a thousand times, and arrange the bread pieces just so.

"Will you marry me?" he blurted out. She looked up at him, amused. "If you keep chopping wood without a shirt, I might take you up on that offer," she replied off-the-cuff. Her hand flew to her mouth, and her eyes bulged in horror. "I'm so sorry, did I just say that out loud?" she said, fleeing the room with the basket of bread before he could reply.

Jake was terribly pleased with himself. He'd been about to apologize for the faux pas, and there she was with a sassy comeback. With a spring in his step, he loaded pasta and sauce into his bowl. She came back and did the same. *Let the flirting begin.*

Once they were seated at the dinner table, Jake asked if she wanted wine, and she said yes. He filled both glasses and then raised his for a toast.

"To holidays by the sea," he said simply with a twinkle in his eye.

"I'll drink to that," said Abby and took a long sip of wine.

Abby

THEY DUG in and ate in silence for a few minutes. It was a comfortable silence.

"Abby, this is amazing," said Jake, finally coming up for air.

"Thanks. There's nothing like fresh tomatoes and herbs to make a sauce pop," she replied, pleased with the compliment. Her last boyfriend had been a decent cook in his own right and rarely complimented her on her dishes. He rarely complimented her on anything. He just assumed that she knew where he stood. She wasn't needy, but all women liked to be told they were pretty once in a while.

Jake hadn't come out and said he thought she was pretty, but it was written all over his face. She didn't know if it was the heat in his gaze or the wine, but she was warm all over. She commented on his business card to steer the conversation to a neutral subject.

"You're a hedge fund manager? I confess I don't know what that is. I know it has to do with investments and the like, but that's about it," she said with a shrug.

He laughed and gave her a quick rundown of his work and firm.

"Things must be going well if you can take off for two weeks and let them fend for themselves!" she said, impressed. She'd had enough of the pasta and bread and was slowly finishing her glass of wine.

"They are. I've worked hard setting up the firm and hiring the best people. I trust them to do as good a job, or even better than I would," he replied, refilling her glass when it was near empty. No one was driving tonight.

The wine was delicious, so she didn't object. One glass was usually her limit.

"What about you? What do you do for work?" he asked, filling his own with the last of the bottle.

"I used to volunteer at the local library, but I gave notice when I sold the house. I guess that makes me unemployed," she said with a laugh.

"Did you work before you had kids?" he asked, looking genuinely interested.

"Paul, my ex-husband, and I met in high school. I had good grades in most of my classes but had no idea what I wanted to do with my life other than getting married and having kids. Paul, on the other hand, had great ambitions. He wanted to become a pharmacist, then manage his independent pharmacy. We married right after prom and moved to Biddeford near the University of New England, where he'd been accepted on a partial scholarship. I registered for a Business Management degree at York Community College. We figured it was a good choice to run a pharmacy when Paul finished his doctorate. I was hired right out of school by an insurance company in South Portland. I worked there for five years while Paul finished school and then worked a year as an associate pharmacist in Scarborough to gain experience. We started shopping for pharmacies in Maine and found the perfect one in Bangor. The owner and his wife were retiring and willing to stay on for three months to help show us the ropes. We bought the house I just sold and moved to Bangor. About a year and a half later, I gave birth to the twins," she said.

"Wow, you have been busy. You didn't want to get back into management after the kids had started school?" he asked.

"I think pregnancy and taking care of babies 24/7 turns your brains to mush. When they started school, and I came up for air, I couldn't imagine doing as good a job as I had before the kids. Besides, I was never passionate about management. It was a means to an end. When I started at the library, I found I was more passionate about books—specifically novels. Like many, I dreamed of writing the all-American novel but never found the time. But now I've got nothing but time," she laughed.

He didn't laugh. Instead, he leaned in closer and asked, "What kind of novels would you write?"

She hesitated. She hadn't told anyone what she truly wanted to do. This might be the perfect opportunity to say it out loud. She didn't know Jake and would likely never see him again. If he thought she was crazy, who cared. She bit her lip and said, "I want to write murder mystery novels, you know, like the ones with Miss Marple. I've never told anyone," she admitted.

"Your secret is safe with me. However, I don't see why it needs to be a secret. I think it's an awesome idea!" he replied enthusiastically.

"You do?" she laughed. "It's not a secret, per se. I've just never told anyone about it before," she replied.

"Well, I'm honored you chose to tell me. Bobbi has shelves upon shelves of mystery novels in her cabin if you need inspiration. I'll loan you a few after dessert." They finished their wine and went to the kitchen to wash the dishes.

Again, they worked in companionable silence until Jake said, "So tell me about your kids." He took a plate she had washed, dried it, and put it away. It was odd doing dishes in a man's kitchen. She was grateful for the question. If there was one thing Abby could do endlessly, it was talk about her kids.

"Kim and Kyle are the best kids a woman could have. People would tell me that having twins was a nightmare, but that hasn't been my experience. Sure, they were a handful as babies and toddlers. When I count my blessings at night, I thank God that Paul waited until the kids were in preschool before he left. We had our differences, but I wouldn't have made it without him those first three years," she said, remembering how she had thought they had made a great team caring for their kids. And they had. They had forgotten how to be a couple, which had prompted Paul to seek solace in the arms of their assistant manager, Mandy.

Abby had felt like such a fool, especially since she had told all the ladies at the Mommy and Me group that theirs was a blessed relationship. She had honestly thought everything was okay between them. Sure, they didn't have sex quite as often as before the kids had arrived, but all couples went through that when they had children. She expected things to spice up once the babies started sleeping through the night. And they had, for a while. She had finally gotten a handle on the household, and she wasn't so tired. They'd even found a pair of babysitters that someone had recommended. She was sure things were going better. Until the day Bailey Simpson told her she'd seen Paul kissing Mandy in broad daylight by the pharmacy's back door.

Abby didn't know what hurt more; the fact that Paul was cheating on her or the fact that Bailey had told her within earshot of their whole group of friends. The looks of pity on their faces as Abby had first tried to deny it. And the blow when her close friend Poppy had confirmed seeing them the month before. The woman who Abby had thought of as her closest friend had known about Paul's extramarital affairs for a month and hadn't said a thing. The betrayal had been too much for Abby to bear, and she'd severed ties with the lot of them, vowing to make her marriage work no matter the cost.

She never had time to implement any of her plans because Paul came clean and told her that he wanted a divorce that very night. He was very nice about it but made it very clear that he was in love with Mandy, and nothing she could say or do would change his mind. He dropped his second bombshell minutes later. Mandy was pregnant, and they moved to New Jersey to be close to her family.

"I promise to take care of you and the kids. You'll never lack for anything, and we'll figure out a custody arrangement that's in everyone's best interest," he had said as Abby had slowly sunk to the floor in shock.

Jake's voice made her jump out of her memories. They had finished the dishes, and he was looking at her intently, the dishrag dangling from his hands.

"Are you okay? You looked like you were miles away for a minute there," he said with concern etched on his face.

She pulled the corners of her mouth into a smile and assured him everything was fine.

"Are you ready to head to my place? I'd put on some pants and bring a sweater if I were you. Once the sun sets, it'll be cold out by the water," he advised.

Abby ran up to change into jeans and a t-shirt, grabbing a hoodie for later. She also put on some socks and grabbed her hiking shoes. She'd been walking with her sandals all week and hadn't had a chance to wear them yet.

He was waiting for her by the door. Though it was almost eight, it was still light out. There was no need to hurry, the sun wouldn't set for another half hour, and they followed the path to the west beach to watch the sun's progression as they made their way to the cabin.

Abby got another pang of regret that she would miss out on buying the island. *Imagine taking a sunset stroll on your very own island*. It would be the perfect place to write a novel, undisturbed.

When they got to the cabin, Jake asked if she wanted to see it while he made coffee and scooped out the cobbler. Abby admitted she was curious to see the inside of the little log cabin.

It was a charming one-room cabin with a murphy bed. Jake showed her the bookshelf, and Abby immediately started choosing a few she hadn't read yet. They took their coffee and cobbler out to the dock and sat in the two Adirondack chairs. It was almost time. The sky was every shade of pink, orange, and red. It was truly magical.

She turned to look at Jake to see if he was as awed as she was. He looked in awe, but he hadn't been looking at the sunset. She blushed like a schoolgirl and turned back to look out at the water. Absently, she started eating the cobbler. It was good. It would have been even better with vanilla ice cream, but she could see how that was the kind of delicacy that was hard to come by on an island. Without a cooler, it might melt on the way back from the grocery store.

"This *is* a treat! First the sunset and now this cobbler! Your mamma raised you right, son!" she exclaimed with a faux southern accent, which had Jake laughing out loud.

Jake

~~~

MOTHERFUCKER! thought Jake as he listened to Abby's story. From what he gathered, she had put herself through a two-year college program she wasn't interested in, put her husband through six years of pharm school, and helped him start his business. He had repaid her hard work by running out on her and the twins to shack up with another woman and move to another state. *What a dick move!* Jake wanted to punch the son-of-a-bitch.

What made him even angrier was that Abby told it like it had been a walk in the park. She didn't seem to bear her ex any ill-will. She had to be a saint. No wonder she was so independent and competent. She'd raised two kids by herself for the past fifteen years. Maybe she'd been bitter those first few years and had gotten over it by now, which would account for her very detached explanation. That's why he hadn't shared his thoughts with her. He couldn't trust himself not to start throwing dishes instead of putting them away in the cupboard.

He got a few minutes to himself while she ran up to change. He took deep breaths and told himself to let it go. Things had obviously worked out for her and the kids, at least financially, if she had never gone back to work and was planning on buying his island to write mystery novels. More power to her. He hoped she had taken that two-timing asshole to the cleaners in the divorce. He caught himself then. He might be overreacting to her situation because of the slight parallel with his own. But there was no contest. He vowed to stop feeling sorry for himself. As bad as it had felt to be left at the altar, he had dodged a bullet there.

Now he felt bad for her. Not because of her ordeal, but because he knew he wasn't going to sell her the island. She'd be homeless because of him. When the two weeks were up, he promised himself he'd do everything in his power to help her out, even and especially if she said she would be fine.

When they got to Bobbi's cabin, he offered to show her around. But once inside, he realized he hadn't put the bed back in the wall. He'd made the bed; he wasn't a neanderthal. But it gave the cozy cabin an intimate feel with her in it. She didn't comment on it and scooted around the bed to select some novels to read from Bobbi's collection.

Out on the deck, she'd caught him staring at her instead of the sunset. He'd seen countless sunsets, but he'd never met a woman like Abby; a business degree, a great cook, a fantastic mom. And she must have an adventurous spirit to be considering living on an off-grid island by herself. Not to mention she could sit quietly and not feel the need to fill the silence. He wished he'd met her sooner.

He couldn't help the pride that swelled in his heart; not only at the compliment on his cobbler, but at the sweet smile he had managed to paint on her lips.

They chatted a while longer after the sun had set. Jake got her talking about her kids some more, and it was fully dark when they heard the first rumble of thunder from out at sea. Jake took the dishes into the house and placed them in the sink before walking Abby back to the main house.

It had felt entirely natural to take her hand on the short walk back. She was so easy to be with. It felt like she'd always been there, cooking meals in his kitchen, cutting herbs from his garden, sneaking her way into his heart.

She hadn't pulled her hand out of his, not even when they'd walked up the porch steps. He was on the verge of kissing her good night, but he lost his nerve and took a step back, letting their fingers drift apart. It was too soon. Christ, he should have been on his honeymoon. He clamped down on those thoughts and plastered a smile on his face.

"Thanks for dinner, Abby. It was the best I've had in a long while," he said easily.

"You're welcome. Thanks for the cobbler and the magical sunset. I can't imagine you ever get tired of it," she replied.

"I don't. I admit, seeing it from Bobbi's cabin was a new experience for me this week, and I'm happy I got to share it with you," he said, realizing he was sincere.

"Okay, then. Thanks again. Good night, Jake," she said through the screen door.

"Good night, Abby. Sleep tight," he replied before she closed the inner door.

He made it back to the cabin just before the downpour started.

Abby

ABBY HAD SLEPT LIKE A LOG. She stretched lazily in bed and looked out the window. It was pouring rain. She debated going back to sleep, but it was already nine. She slipped into her robe and made her way down the stairs.

She padded to the kitchen and put the coffee on. She poured a cup and took it upstairs when the coffee was ready. It was too cold and windy to go up to the widow's walk, so she stood in front of the patio doors and looked out at the raging sea.

The storm was really picking up. The water in the bay was choppy, and she could see the boat bobbing up and down, hitting the deck in a way that had her worried it might break.

The wind had picked up, and she nearly jumped out of her skin when a flying branch hit the window. She screamed and dropped her cup to the floor. The cup shattered. Annoyed with her own clumsiness, she went back downstairs to get a rag, a broom, and a dustpan.

Once she'd picked up the mess, she went back down for another cup of coffee. She should carry this one back to bed and snuggle in with a book. It was clearly not a day to be out and about.

Once she was back in bed, hands warming around the coffee cup, she had difficulty concentrating on her book. Her gaze kept being pulled to the storm outside. The rain was now hitting the windows and making a tap, tap, tapping noise. She wondered if it was hailing, but it was now raining sideways. *Wait*, she thought, *isn't that one of the signs of a hurricane?* If it were, there'd be an alert on her phone. Damn. It was downstairs in the office nook. With a sigh, she threw off the blankets, stuffed her arms back into her robe, and grudgingly went down the stairs. On the upside, she was getting some steps in.

She nearly missed the last step and yelped when she heard the loudest clap of thunder she had ever heard. The lightning struck close to the house, and she saw a man standing with an ax through the door window.

When she heard loud banging, she screamed.

Jake

JAKE WOKE up well past his usual hour. He heard the rain clattering on the metal roof. It was a soothing sound and likely the reason he had overslept. He debated going for a run. The clap of thunder quickly squashed that idea.

He got up, made coffee, and went through the motions of doing a few push-ups and sit-ups just so he didn't feel so lazy when he went back to bed. He grabbed his book and marveled at his own laziness. He stared out at the sea for a while, mesmerized by the endless drops of rain on the surface.

Jake's head shot up when his phone buzzed with a text. Thinking it might be Abby, he got up to retrieve it from the kitchen counter. It wasn't Abby. It was an emergency alert. Hurricane Gunther Warning. Scrolling through his texts, he saw there had been a Hurricane Watch overnight, and he'd missed it. He swore under his breath, not because he was worried. The island had weathered storms and hurricanes valiantly in the past. And he knew they had a little time before it hit. No, he swore because Abby might not know that and was likely to panic when she got the alert. He was about to call her but then thought better of it. He would need to go over there anyway to put the emergency plan into motion. And if she hadn't seen the alert, he didn't want to worry her before he got there.

He got dressed, stuffed his things in a backpack, and closed up the cabin. It wasn't safe to be this close to the water. He put the perishables into Bobbi's cooler, packed the rest of the food in a large reusable grocery bag, and made his way to the big house.

When he knocked on the door, he heard a blood-curdling scream and swore under his breath. He should have called or texted Abby before coming over.

"Abby, are you okay?" he called to her. The rain was so loud that he couldn't hear her response. He was about to use his key when the door swung open, and she let him inside.

"What are you doing out in the rain? You scared me half to death!" she said, her face ashen.

"I'm sorry, did I wake you?" he said, shaking off the excess water and putting down the cooler and grocery bag. He removed his backpack but kept his coat on.

"No, but I was only just coming down the steps and saw your silhouette in the door window. I thought you were an ax murder!" she said.

"I'm sorry I scared you. Have you checked your phone?" he asked.

"No, that's what I came down for, to check if there was a storm warning," she replied and made to go and get it.

He grabbed her arm lightly to stop her. "I'll save you the trouble. There was a Hurricane Watch alert last night, and about thirty minutes ago, there was a Hurricane Warning alert. We have time, but we do have to prepare," he said, keeping his voice steady to reassure her.

"Okay, what should I do?" she asked, her eyes round as saucers.

"For now, could you put this food away?" he asked. When she nodded, he added, "I'll go out and secure the guest house and the other outbuildings. When I get back, you can help me put the shutters on the windows," he said as he opened the door.

"Okay, I'll get dressed. I'll be ready," she said and was putting the food away when he left.

Abby

ABBY WENT to check her phone. Besides the alerts, she'd gotten a text from both her kids. They had texted back and forth a few times that week. She told them about the storm, that all was well, and that she would be in touch in a few days, assuming she still had cell service. She didn't want them to worry. Since both her phone and laptop were fully charged, she unplugged them to avoid any surges there might be during the storm.

She went up to change, throwing on the same clothes she'd had on last night, and brought her coat down. She'd seen some old rain boots in the storage closet and went to get those. They might prove handier than her hiking boots in the mud and rain. She placed them by the door and went to peer out the window in the dining room, trying to catch a glimpse of Jake. He was heading back to the house. She put on her coat, slipped into the boots, and met him on the porch.

"We have colonial shutters on the first floor," he said, shouting to be heard above the rain. "They're pretty easy, just fold them in and close the latch." He demonstrated on the window by the door. She nodded and went in the opposite direction. They met at the back of the house once all the windows were secure. The wind was picking up, the rain had intensified, and the temperature had dropped. Despite the slicker and the boots, Abby was drenched.

"We have rolling shutters on the upper floor. Come on, I'll show you," he said, and they went back in the house. They removed their coats and boots, and Abby could feel the chill inside the house as well. She shuddered and rubbed her arms.

"Let's get the shutters done, and then we can change into dry clothes," said Jake.

With the shutters in place, it was dark inside the house. Jake took a flashlight from inside his coat pocket, and they made their way upstairs. He showed Abby how to roll down and lock the shutters. It was easy and quickly done. They didn't linger in the darkened bedroom and were soon back in the living room.

"What's next?" she asked.

"Now, we wait," he said. Then, when she started fidgeting, he added, "The house, the boat, and outbuildings are secure. The solar panels are strong and should withstand even the worst hurricane."

"But won't we run out of power from the lack of sunshine?" asked Abby.

"No, the panels still catch indirect sunlight. If we refrain from unnecessary use, the panels will power the important stuff for quite a few stormy days," he answered.

"So, no Netflix?" she joked, and he nodded with a smile. "Have you had breakfast yet?" she asked. It was almost eleven by then, and she was starving.

She took out a bowl. She was taking out the carton of eggs to make an omelet when she stopped. "Should we make an inventory? Maybe ration our food?" she asked earnestly.

He shook his head. "We have more than enough fresh food to last the next week. The worst of even a category five hurricane will be over by then. In all likelihood, we're in for a rocky twenty-four to forty-eight hours at the most," he said.

Abby turned to look out of the window, only to remember all the windows were boarded up. The wind was howling outside, and she could hear the rain beating against the window. She didn't like not being able to see out. Though Jake had made it clear they would be safe, warm, and well-fed throughout the storm, and she believed him, she wasn't a fan of the dark. She'd read too many novels and couldn't help an involuntary shudder as she imagined a maniac lying in wait.

"Are you cold?" asked Jake, concern etched in his features. "I really think you should get out of those wet clothes. Maybe consider a hot shower," he added.

Abby laughed and replied, "It does feel a little damp, but honestly, I was just scaring myself with horror stories in my head."

"Why don't I start a fire. It'll chase away the chill and light up the living room, so it's not so dark," he said.

When she didn't move, he asked, "Is there anything else bothering you?"

Abby stared at her feet. It was humiliating to admit that a grown woman could be afraid of the dark.

Jake came closer and gently put a finger under her chin, forcing her to look at him. "Abby, it's going to be all right. I've been through my share of storms and hurricanes and have lived to tell the tale," he said with a reassuring smile.

His tone was gentle and soothing, like he was talking to a child. But Abby didn't feel like a child. She felt like a woman. Though his shirt was as wet as hers, he was giving off heat that was doing more than warming up her body. It was warming her blood. She was suddenly acutely aware that her nipples, which had managed to stay put despite the chill, were now fully erect and peeking through her flimsy bra and damp t-shirt. The shiver that ran through her body just then wasn't from the cold. It was pure lust.

Their eyes locked. And, at that moment, she would have told him anything, even her most secret desires. Thankfully, she did not blurt out her current thought, which screamed, *Take me!* Instead, she said, "I don't want to shower in the dark."

"Come here," he said and pulled her in against him, rubbing her back and arms. It was clearly a hug meant to reassure her and warm her up. It felt amazing. She wrapped her arms around his waist and hung onto him like he was the last man alive, inhaling his tantalizing aroma that had driven her to distraction on the day she had arrived. She sighed in contentment.

"Better?" he asked as he pulled away. She nodded, reluctantly releasing him and feeling a little embarrassed for clinging to him the way she had.

"I got you covered," he said, tapping the tip of her nose and heading into the dining room. He could obviously see in the dark. Then again, this was his house, and he likely knew where things were. He came back with two oil lamps and some matches. He lit them both and gave one of them to Abby.

"Thank you," she said gratefully and headed upstairs.

Jake

JAKE SHOOK his head as he got the fire going. Who would have thought that super-efficient Abby would be afraid of the dark? It was adorable. The way she had clung to him when he was hugging her, however, was not. When their eyes locked, he had felt the shift. He'd only meant to reassure her. Hurricanes were scary, even for those who'd lived through them. The level of destruction they could wreak in such a short time was nothing short of phenomenal.

But at that moment, instinct had taken over. The scared and vulnerable look in her eyes had turned dark and hungry in an instant. He'd barely touched her, his finger under her chin being the only point of contact. It was the look in her eyes that had turned the heat up so high he thought he'd combust on the spot. He did the only thing he could think of to break the spell. This was no time to be getting hot and heavy.

As he pulled her into his arms, he felt her hard nipples poking against his abdomen, and he groaned inwardly. What had started as a quick hug to warm and reassure had turned hotter than hell when she wrapped her arms around him and squeezed. He had to let go before he embarrassed both of them with a massive erection.

He'd given her an oil lamp and sent her up to shower and change.

Once the fire was going, he got his backpack and went to shower in the downstairs bathroom. Part of him needed a cold shower, and he took care of it while he had some privacy. As tension drained out of him, he relaxed under the hot spray and prayed he could keep his hands to himself for the time they would be stuck together.

When he got out of the bathroom, he heard her puttering in the kitchen. She was frying bacon and scrambling some eggs. He joined her in the kitchen and made a fresh pot of coffee. When the toast popped, he took out a couple of plates and placed two pieces on each plate. He put two more in for later.

"How do you take your coffee?" he asked when it was ready. She was dividing the eggs and bacon between their plates by now, putting more on his. Great. He was starving.

"Cream and sugar, please," she replied and set their plates on the island in front of the stools. He filled their cups, added cream and sugar to hers, and placed the cups next to their dishes. She had already set jam, butter, and other assorted condiments, so he got the utensils and a couple of napkins.

"Let's eat!" he said, and they sat side by side to enjoy their feast.

Abby ground out some salt and pepper onto her eggs and barely had time to turn her head into her arm before letting out a gigantic sneeze.

"Bless you," said Jake, taking the pepper mill out of her hands. "Are you getting sick?" he asked.

Abby waved a hand at him, "No, I'm never sick. It's probably just the pepper."

But when she reached for the sliced tomatoes, three more sneezes came out in quick succession. Jake went to get the box of tissues from the bathroom and placed them in front of her.

"A lot of people get sick while on vacation," said Jake. "Especially those who never get sick. We were out in the rain for a while. You probably caught a chill," he added.

Abby narrowed her eyes at him like he was responsible for making her sick, or perhaps she was about to disagree with him. She grabbed a tissue and stepped away to blow her nose. It wasn't the dainty nose dabbing he'd seen Jen do after she'd been crying. No, this was an all-out honk. Jake held his laughter as she tossed out the used tissue, washed her hands, and came back to the table.

She was still scowling when she sat down and started stabbing her eggs. Jake brought the tomatoes near her, and she impaled them with such force that they slipped right off of her fork. He tipped the plate and let them slide onto hers. *Interesting.* Abby was a grumpy sick person. The kind who didn't like to show weakness. That was even more adorable than being afraid of the dark. And here he had thought she was too perfect to be human.

She mumbled her thanks, and they ate in silence for a few minutes. Hoping to distract her, both from the storm and her imminent cold, Jake asked about her hobbies since she had mentioned she enjoyed walking. She told him she loved to hike and went out every chance she got.

"I've got all the Maine 4,000-footers crossed off my list except for the two on Katahdin: Baxter and Hamlin Peaks. They require a little more planning, as you need to reserve your spot in advance, and I'm not the kind of hiker who'll head up a major peak in the pouring rain. So, I tend to head out at the last minute when I'm sure the weather will collaborate," she explained. "Do you hike? What are your hobbies?" she asked.

It was easy getting her to talk, and so far, Jake had been able to maneuver the conversation away from his personal life. This was an innocent enough question to answer.

"Since my job requires a lot of focus, I like to do things that are relaxing in my downtime. I like to read, fish, and I jog to stay fit," he said.

"Don't forget berry picking and gardening," quipped Abby.

"Picking berries reminds me of the days I spent here as a boy. My grandmother and later my mom did the gardening, while my grandfather and my dad took care of the land and chores. Now, it all falls to Bobbi, though I admit I enjoyed taking on the chores this week. I can see why Bobbi likes it. At the end of the day, you've got a clear idea of what you've accomplished," he said.

Abby nodded, seeming lost in her thoughts. "I read somewhere that there is a higher incidence of job-related burnout in white-collar workers compared to blue-collar workers. That must be why," she said. Then she added, "I got a lot more out of raising my kids and taking care of my home than I ever did while managing insurance claims. It was a little better when I was running the drug store because it was ours and because I knew we were making a difference in the community."

"I get that. I was so focused on getting ahead and making money in my thirties that I didn't notice the toll it was taking on my health and well-being until I started my own firm and things started to calm down. All of a sudden, I had all this free time and no one to share it with," he said. They'd both finished eating, so he took their plates and brought them to the sink. Abby finished her cup of coffee and brought over the cups, and they started on the dishes.

"I thought I was doing the right thing, waiting until I was established before settling down with a wife and kids. I wanted a hand in raising my kids, to be there for them, and to support my wife, more than just as a provider," continued Jake as he washed while Abby dried.

"I wish more men thought like that," she said. "Even if Paul had stuck around, I doubt he'd have been home much. It's a lot of work starting a business. We waited a few years before starting our family, but it doesn't change the fact that it's a hectic part of life. Men can afford to wait a bit," she said before another round of sneezes overtook her.

Jake looked at her then. She was flushed and didn't look well at all. He was sure she would balk if he suggested she go upstairs for a nap. No, he'd have to be sneaky about it. When they were done with the dishes, he suggested they sit in the living room by the fire.

"You don't mind if I read, do you? I'm halfway through a John Grisham novel, and I'm dying to know what happens next," he said.

"Not at all. I'll do the same. What are you reading?" she asked while he rummaged through his backpack.

He showed her the cover of *Camino Winds* and sat down in the armchair.

"That's a good one. Have you read *Camino Island*?" Abby asked.

"Yeah, that's why I pounced on this one when I saw it in Bobbi's collection," he replied.

"I'll run up and get my book," she said but stopped when she reached the stairs. She seemed to be swaying slightly. Jake was up in a flash and put a hand on her back to steady her. He steered her back towards the sofa and pushed her down into the cushions. The fact that she didn't put up a fight or make any snarky comments was proof that she was unwell.

Jake put his hand on her forehead. "Abby, you're burning up," he said. "Lie down, and I'll make you some tea."

Abby

AFTER THE STRING OF SNEEZES, Abby had to admit to herself, if not to Jake, that she might be coming down with a cold. She could feel the tickle at the back of her throat and the headache forming behind her eyes. She hated being sick; it made one so ineffective. Then again, this was the perfect time to be unproductive. Especially with the storm raging outside; she literally had nothing better to do than rest and wait it out.

Under the guise of getting her book, she would pop a couple of pain relievers, but she never made it upstairs. She'd barely put her hand on the railing when she started feeling faint. Jake was immediately at her side, though she swore she had seen him settle into the armchair by the fire with his book. She must not have been hiding her discomfort all that well if he'd been keeping an eye on her.

As she sank into the cushions of the sofa, she felt her bones dissolve, and in the time it took for Jake to brew the tea, she was out.

She woke later feeling sweaty and disoriented. There was a cloth on her forehead that might have been cool at one time but now felt heavy and warm. She removed it and tried to sit up. She couldn't manage it and groaned in defeat.

Jake came into her line of vision. "How are you feeling?" he asked, crouching down to face her. He took the cloth from her hands and placed it in a bowl on the coffee table. He wrung out the excess water and positioned the cloth back on her forehead.

Abby sighed in audible relief. "Better now that you've calmed the inferno," she mumbled.

Jake took the cloth and sponged her face and neck before returning it to the bowl and back to her forehead.

"You're running a fever, and you passed out before I could give you the tea. It's my grandmother's recipe. You'll feel better if you have a cup. Do you think you can sit up?" he asked as he placed a hand under her shoulder to lift her. When she started sinking back towards the sofa, he held her in place and propped her up with added pillows.

He brought the cup to her lips, and she took a sip. "Mmm," she said and drank down the whole cup. "What's in this?" she asked.

"It's a blend of ginger, catnip leaf, yarrow flowers, peppermint leaf, chamomile flowers, cinnamon, and a bit of honey," he replied.

"Is there more?" she asked when he took her empty cup. He handed her a glass of water instead. "There is, but you should wait a few hours before your next dose if you still feel poorly," he said.

She took a few sips of water and found she was parched. Once she'd drained the water, he took the glass and placed it on the coffee table.

"How long was I out for?" she asked.

Jake checked his watch and replied, "We finished breakfast at about noon, and it's now two-thirty."

"Wow," said Abby, "that's quite a nap."

She felt a little better but found she still couldn't sit up independently. She was happy only the fireplace illuminated the room; her eyes hurt, and the light would have been murder. She massaged her forehead and temples.

"You should feel better soon. I would have carried you up to the bedroom so you'd be more comfortable, but I didn't want you to wake up alone. It's pretty dark up there," he said.

Abby groaned inwardly this time, remembering the heated exchange in the dining room. She flushed when she thought of how she'd yearned for him to kiss her even though she knew it was a bad idea. Having sex with Jake would undoubtedly be a great way to pass the time and keep her mind off the storm.

Thankfully, fate had stepped in before she could make a fool of herself. As much as she hated being sick, she would be a lot worse for wear if she'd yielded to her baser instincts. There was no question that they had a mutual attraction. On the surface, she could see how they'd do well together. They had a lot in common; they were both avid readers who enjoyed the outdoors. They were both independent and kept their own company. And they both had a lot of free time to devote to a budding relationship.

However, Abby doubted they would be a good fit in the long run. Aside from being heartbroken about his recent breakup, Jake was adamant about having kids. Though she wasn't too old to have more children, Abby had no interest in giving up her newfound freedom. She'd raised her kids and sent them off into the world as responsible, well-adjusted young adults. She had done a great job, and it was time to focus on her own life. Though she'd love a committed relationship, she was hoping to meet someone who wanted the same things she wanted: to travel, see the world, and go on adventures.

Abby had to be smart. She was leaving in a week and couldn't afford to give her heart to the first hot guy that gave her the time of day. Though she liked Jake, she really didn't know that much about him. So far, he'd gotten her to spill most of her life story, but he had yet to share any intimate details.

She knew he was solid and hardworking. Despite having a white-collar job, he seemed to have a well-rounded life. He was fit, took time to unwind by reading and fishing, and enjoyed being outdoors and tending to the land. And he knew how to take care of someone with a cold. For now, those were enough to build a friendship.

"Tell me about yourself," she said, turning to her side to look at him. He'd gone back to the armchair and was loosely holding his book. "Unless you want to read?" she added.

He looked around for something to place inside his book. He reached for one of the newspapers by the fireplace, tore a piece, and used it as a bookmark. Abby was happy to see he wasn't the kind of heathen who would dog-ear the pages of a book. It said a lot about him.

"What do you want to know?" he asked as he put the book on the side table.

Jake

ABBY ASKED if he had any close friends. This was a safe enough topic, and he told her about Trent and his little family.

"Trent and I met in college, and we've been as close as brothers ever since. When I started the firm, I tried to get Trent to partner with me. At the time, he and Rosie were newly married and wanted to start a family. He had a good job in one of the bigger firms, which didn't require as much energy and focus as starting something new would have required. I got that. Now that he's just had his fourth child, I might give it another try. Especially since the place mostly runs itself now. I guess we'll see how it goes once they've settled into a routine with the new baby," he said.

Abby had been paying attention, but he could see her eyelids drooping and eventually flutter closed. He chuckled. His boring life had put her to sleep. He watched her sleep for a little while. She really was a stunning woman. In repose, her face was at peace, the worry lines smoothed from her brow. She wore a contented smile like she had enjoyed listening to him before falling asleep. When her breathing evened out, he gently removed one of the pillows so her neck wouldn't be sore and readjusted the blanket that had fallen to her waist. He couldn't help pushing back the curls that had fallen over her face. His fingers brushed her skin. It was soft and not as warm as it had been before. *Good*, he thought; the fever was reducing. She'd feel a lot better when she woke. When she did, he could distract her with a board game.

He added a log to the fire and settled back in the armchair to read his book but found he had difficulty concentrating now. He resisted the urge to check on the storm. There would be damage and debris, but the important stuff was tied down, and he hadn't heard anything come crashing against the house. That was another positive thing about being on a private island; they wouldn't be picking up neighbors' debris in their yard. With every storm, you learned what worked and what didn't, and you made improvements accordingly.

Jake took in his surroundings and let out a sigh of contentment. He was blessed, and he knew it. The house was not only keeping them safe, but it was also beautiful and comfortable. He had everything he needed right here on the island.

His gaze fell on the sleeping woman on his couch. Somehow, she fits here too. Like she'd always been here. Once the storm had passed, he would need to head back to Bobbi's cabin. Sure, they would cross paths and perhaps share a meal or two before she had to leave. Where would she go? He felt like he needed more time to get to know her like he'd be missing out on something important if she left. Theirs was a budding friendship with an obvious attraction. Would that be enough to convince her to stay?

Was he ready to jump in so soon after the fiasco with Jen? If he were honest, he'd barely given Jen another thought in the last couple of days. Sure, he still wanted kids, and Abby was clear she was done with all that. But unfortunately, she was likely to get grandkids before he could find someone to have kids with. Men couldn't just decide to have kids on their own. Well, he guessed they could with an assist from technology or adoption.

Trent had jokingly said Jake was welcome to borrow his kids anytime he felt like playing daddy. But it wasn't the same as the bond you developed with your own child. True, he was Max's godfather, Trent and Rosie's eldest. But, so far, that hadn't translated into much as the boy was only five. Perhaps as he got older, Jake could take a more active role in his life, show him how to fish, track animals, and pick wild berries. Would that be enough?

Trent had also suggested he volunteer as a Big Brother. "There are so many ways to contribute to a child's well-being without being a parent. You might serve an even more important role in a child's life by being a friend, a mentor, or a role model. Parents are often tired and overwhelmed, and kids rarely get the attention and affection they need. You could be the deciding factor in how a kid turns out," Trent had said.

Jake had said he would look into it, but he hadn't. This was before he had gotten engaged to Jen, and he didn't want to commit to someone else's child if he was about to have one of his own and have a split focus. If he had a child, he would be all-in. With Jen gone, he was back to square one. It might be time to revisit the idea and check out the website to see what being a Big Brother actually involved. He'd never made it that far.

Jake felt the tightness in his chest loosen. He wasn't giving up on having kids, but he was letting go of the struggle. The situation was out of his control, and there was no sense in crying over spilled milk, as his grandma used to say. He had something to offer to the next generation, and he now had multiple ways to transmit his knowledge that he could implement as soon as he got back to the city.

Better yet, he'd try a little one-on-one with Max when Trent came to the island with his family later in the month. Maybe he'd get a tiny fishing pole from the mainland. With the new baby, the boy might enjoy a little more attention. Yes, that's what he would do. If he couldn't hook him into fishing, he was sure to get him with the berries.

Abby stirred. She was mumbling in her sleep and kicking her feet. Jake could see she was flushed and sweaty. Guessing the fever was spiking, he went to refill her cup with tea and add cool water to the basin he was using to cool her down. She didn't wake up when he wiped her brow, face, and neck with the cool cloth, but she seemed to settle. He wrung it out and placed it on her forehead.

An angel had fallen into his lap right when he needed her. Jake studied the sleeping beauty. Her chestnut hair was a tangled mess on the cushion, and though he'd wiped the sheen of sweat from her face, her cheeks still held that rosy glow from the fever. She was a good ten years older than Jen, the evidence of which could be seen in the lines around her eyes and mouth. But he was sure he'd never seen a more beautiful woman.

He was still crouching near her face when she opened her eyes.

Abbey

ABBY WAS HAVING A NIGHTMARE. Her babies were crying, and she couldn't reach them. The faster she ran, the further they seemed to get. Meanwhile, the wolves chasing her were gaining on her. She tripped on a root and fell. In an instant, the pack leader was on her. She bucked and kicked, but she couldn't dislodge him. Her hand shot up under its chin, hoping to keep him from biting, but that left his paws free to scratch at her.

Suddenly, a mountain lion came out of nowhere and rammed into the wolf so hard the beast flew through the air and landed on its side, panting. The mountain lion got between her and the wolf and growled, planting its paws firmly while advancing slowly to show the other who was boss.

The wolf soon cowered and ran in the opposite direction, the pack following in his wake. The massive cat sniffed her from head to toe as though scanning for injuries and started licking her wounds one by one, ending with the burning scratches on her face and neck. It was weird, but it felt good. Once he was done, her protector lay down beside her and let her rest. She felt safe while her wounds healed. She would get up soon; her babies needed her.

At the thought of her babies, Abby opened her eyes. The green eyes that greeted her were not those of a mountain lion but Jake's.

"I need to get my babies," she said.

Jake nodded, reached over to grab the cup, and brought it to her lips.

"You need to heal first. Here, have some more of the tea," he said, slipping a hand between her shoulder blades to lift her. Abby took a tentative sip, then remembered this tea was good and placed a hand around the cup and sat up so she could drink it down.

"Easy, now. We don't want you getting light-headed," said Jake, placing another cushion behind her back so she could lay back a bit. The cloth had dropped from her forehead, and he put it in the bowl on the table.

Abby blinked, the nightmare slowly receding to the back of her mind. Jake was sitting on one of the ottomans, keeping vigil at her side. She smiled at him, remembering his role in her dream. "Thank you," she said with a sigh, resting back on the cushions. She was feeling so relaxed. Jake cocked his head, frowned, and placed a hand on her forehead. "How are you feeling? Are you hungry?" he asked.

"What time is it?" she asked. She couldn't seem to lift her arm to check her watch. Checking his own, he replied, "It's a little after four o'clock. We had a big breakfast, but I'm about ready for a snack. How about you?"

"I could eat," she said and made to sit up. Jake placed a hand on her shoulder, keeping her in place.

"If you want to sit up, I'll put another pillow behind you. I don't recommend you getting up just yet," he said, grabbing a cushion and raising an eyebrow in question. She nodded and let him position it behind her.

"Sit tight; I'll warm up some soup and put together some sandwiches, okay?" he asked, getting up. As though reading her mind, he handed her a glass of water before making his way to the kitchen.

Propped up as she was, she could see him in the kitchen. He grabbed a pot, opened a can of soup, and set it on the stove to warm. Next, he rummaged through the fridge and asked if she preferred ham and cheese or an egg salad sandwich.

"Either is fine," she replied.

"I'll make one of each, and we can share," he said. He placed four slices of bread on the cutting board and started to stack the fixings, pausing to ask if she wanted lettuce, then mayonnaise or mustard. He closed the sandwiches, sliced them crosswise, and placed the halves onto their plates. He ladled the soup into mugs and turned off the stove. Checking the cupboards, he grabbed a bag of chips and waved it at her. "Salt and vinegar?" he asked.

"My favorite!" she said, smiling.

He placed a handful on each plate and brought hers on a tray so she could remain on the couch to eat. "It feels like Mother's Day," she said with a laugh.

"Why do you say that?" he asked, heading back with his own cup and plate. He set them down on the placemat on the coffee table. He pulled an ottoman out from under the coffee table and sat facing her.

"That's about the only time anyone makes lunch for me," she said with a shrug.

Jake

COME ON! Jake had half a mind to call her kids and give them a piece of his mind. No wonder she'd gotten sick; she was overworked and underappreciated. He'd made her canned soup and a sandwich, and she was acting like he'd given her a Rolls Royce. Jake wished he could do more for her, but what?

The words were out of his mouth before he'd thought things through.

"You know, you can stay here for as long as you need to sort things out. You don't have to go when the two weeks are up," he suggested, surprising himself.

"That's very generous of you, Jake, but where will you go?" Abby replied in between spoonfuls of soup. She was looking better; hopefully, the fever wouldn't return.

"I'm going to have to stick around and get repairs done after the storm. There's no way I'm leaving the whole mess to Bobbi to clean up when she comes back. I can stay in the Annex," he explained.

She was nibbling half of the sandwich, and he had already wolfed down everything. He got up to get more chips. He offered her some, but she only shook her head.

"If anything, I should be the one to move into the guest house. This is your home, and I'm not even a guest!" she said, trying to put the soup cup on the coffee table, but she was too far to reach.

He got up and took it from her. His fingers brushed hers, and there was an instant spark. He could have chalked it up to static electricity, but he was sure there was more to it. She hadn't let go of the cup, and he was sure he felt her fingers brush his.

What am I, twelve?

"Are you done with the sandwich? I can wrap it up for you and put it in the fridge in case you get hungry later," he suggested. She nodded, let go of the cup, and then gave him her plate.

"I'm asking you to be my guest, Abby," he said softly.

Her eyes met his and held his gaze for a moment. Jake had a hard time reading her expression. Was she checking to see if his invitation was sincere? Did she wonder if he had an ulterior motive?

Do I? Of course, I do. I need more time with her.

She looked away and busied herself with the blanket on her lap.

"Thank you for the offer, Jake. That's very generous. You don't mind if I think about it, do you?" she replied with great diplomacy.

Fair enough.

"Not at all. I just wanted you to know you've got some options," he said over his shoulder as he brought the dishes into the kitchen and put everything away.

"Tea? Coffee?" he asked from the kitchen.

"Just water for me, thanks," she called out to him.

He re-filled her glass and brought back a cup of coffee for himself.

"That smells good. I can't have coffee in the afternoon; it keeps me up at night. And considering I've already caught a few naps today, I might need more of your tea before the night is through," she said.

Outside, the storm escalated, and the windows shook. They could hear the wind howl as it met with resistance. Abby yelped and put the blanket over her head.

Jake resisted the urge to laugh and set his cup on the side table and opened a hidden panel on the coffee table. It was meant for playing board games, and Jake figured they'd likely play a few to pass the time and keep the anxiety down.

"I've got backgammon, chess, checkers, cribbage, or plain old playing cards," exclaimed Jake loudly to be overheard above the storm.

Abby brought the blanket down and blushed in embarrassment. "You must think I'm such a fool," she said. Tentatively, she swung her legs off the sofa and tried to sit up.

"Of course not; storms are loud. I get it," he said.

"Remind me how cribbage works? I think I used to play with my grandma," she said, moving to one of the ottomans like Jake.

They played for a couple of hours, swapping granny stories and family trips up and down the coast of Maine. It got them through the worst of the storm.

Around eight, Abby started to yawn, and they called it quits. Jake asked if she was hungry, but she said no.

If she wasn't eating, then he wasn't going to cook. He heated another can of soup and made himself a tuna fish sandwich. He made Abby another cup of his special tea, but when he brought it all back to the living room, Abby had crept back onto the sofa and was struggling with the blanket.

"Let me get that for you," said Jake rushing over. He covered her with the blanket, then thinking better of it, he scooped her up in his arms and made for the stairs. On his way, he took one of the gas lamps.

Abby, too weak to struggle, could still voice a protest. "What are you doing? Put me down!"

"I get the feeling you're going down for the night, and the couch is no place to get a proper night's rest," he said.

"But I like it in front of the fireplace. It's cozy," she said when he got to the stairs.

When he made no reply and started up, she panicked, and nearly screamed "Stop" near his ear. He stopped halfway up the stairs.

"I don't want to be alone up there," she said, her voice small like a child's.

Jake hung his head. She was afraid of the dark.

"How about I stay with you until you fall asleep. I'll leave the lamp on, and I'll check in on you every hour, I promise," he said, looking down at her. She gave him one of the most trusting looks he'd ever gotten. She swallowed and whispered, "Thank you."

Jake

JAKE KEPT his promise and checked on Abby hourly throughout the night. He was thankful to see that the tea and rest were working, and her fever was getting better. Jake decided that even as her fever broke, she needed to get as much rest as possible. Stress did terrible things to the body and mind. From all she had confessed to him in their short time together, Jake was sure an accumulation of factors was responsible for her condition. She was so strong, but was that how she was naturally? Or was it just her way of suppressing how she truly felt? The storm also scared her, causing additional stress. Add to that the fever itself, and he had no doubt she needed sleep more than anything else.

He headed back downstairs to make a fresh pot of his grandmother's famous tea, listening to the storm outside. It sounded like it was starting to ease. While the wind still howled, the banging from the shutters had stopped a while ago.

Sleep called his name. His eyes had grown heavy, and he yawned, checking his watch. It was three in the morning. He checked in on Abby once more before grabbing a blanket and settling in for the night on the sofa. It wasn't an uncomfortable sofa, but it was still a little cramped for a man of his size. He knew he would wake in the morning with a few new aches and pains.

Sure enough, Jake started the day with a kink in his neck, stretching out and rubbing his new sore spot. He yawned and checked his watch. It was ten-thirty. He quietly popped upstairs to check on Abby. Her face was cool to the touch and starting to regain some of its color. He decided to let her sleep a little longer and headed downstairs.

He made a fresh pot of coffee and planned out his day. First, he needed to see what the storm had done to the property. He went outside and was happy to see minimal damage, nothing he couldn't handle. He started opening the shutters on the lower floor and made a mental note to fix the shutters at the back of the house. They had only stayed attached thanks to the strong latch. Looking around, he noted that only a small amount of clean-up was needed. He could probably get through it all before Bobbi returned.

Heading back inside, he started breakfast. Abby would surely be hungry once she woke. He threw some bacon in a skillet and, while that cooked, fried some eggs after dropping a couple of slices of bread in the toaster. A sound behind him broke him from his task, turning. He saw Abby, still a little groggy, strolling into the kitchen.

"Good morning! How are you feeling?" he asked as he plated up the food.

"Much better, thank you, the smell of food woke me up." She smiled, heading over to the coffee pot as she spoke.

Jake put his hand over hers, stopping her, "Nope, go sit down. I'll bring everything in."

Abby didn't complain. Smiling sweetly, she headed back into the living room.

Shortly after, Jake followed, carrying two plates. He handed Abby hers and placed his on the coffee table before heading back for their coffee.

"Thank you. I'm famished," Abby said as she hungrily tucked into her food. Jake watched as she closed her eyes, a slight grin on her face as she savored and enjoyed every bite.

"Good to see your appetite is back. That's always a good sign," he said, taking a sip of his drink. They ate in silence, simply enjoying the quiet after the storm.

"When did the storm stop?" Abby asked, snuggling into the sofa as she finished, tucking her feet under her.

"Early this morning. I've checked outside, and the damage is minimal," he replied, taking the empty plates and depositing them in the sink. He planned to get to them later.

Neither of them had noticed the cell service had returned until their phones began to ping with multiple missed notifications. Numerous texts and missed calls flashed across both of their screens. Abby checked hers. She had a few texts from her kids. They'd been worrying.

"Oh dear, I better respond to the kids. They must be frantic," she said, tapping away at her screen, and replying to message after message.

Jake said nothing, falling silent when he read the name of the person who had messaged him the most. Jen's name flashed across the screen. *What does she want?* A pang of anger ran through him. It annoyed him that she thought to message him just as he had started to develop feelings for Abby. Finally giving in, he opened the first message.

He froze, holding his breath, his eyes opening ideas. He read the words on the screen.

"Jake? Is everything all right?" Abby asked, her voice laced with concern. Jake didn't answer. Instead, he just stared at his phone, re-reading the message again and again. Abby rested her hand on his knee. The sudden contact broke him from his trance. Looking up at her, the look of worry on her face warmed his heart. *She cares.* He tried to smile but couldn't get the muscles to work. He opened his mouth to speak, but the words simply wouldn't come.

After a moment longer, he decided to tell Abby about his ex. He ran his hands over his face and took a deep breath.

"It's my ex. I haven't heard from her in ten days since she left me at the alter," he said, finally raising his eyes to meet hers.

Her eyes widened in surprise at his sudden honesty, but her eyes urged him to continue, and her hand hadn't left his knee. *It's only fair. She shared so much about her life with me. A gentleman would return the favor,* he thought. Settling in, he told his story, the whirlwind romance, their plans for a family, and her sudden departure. Abby listened intently. It felt so easy talking to her.

"Last I heard, she was spotted boarding her private jet with some Portuguese model," he finished.

"Perhaps she's worried, you know, with the storm," Abby ventured.

Looking up at her, he realized even she knew that was a lie. Jen wanted something. Jake just didn't know what.

"Maybe you should call her. If she has messaged you so many times, it might be important," Abby said softly.

"I don't want to hear anything she has to say," Jake said, trying to hide the hurt and pain in his voice. While he had come to terms with her departure, the event still stung.

Abby looked at him and folded her arms, cocking her right eyebrow.

"Come on now, Jake. You just spent the night taking care – excellent care, I might add – of a woman you barely know. You have a heart of gold. You don't have it in you to be so cold," she said.

Her words finally brought an easy smile to his lips. He liked that she had so much faith in him and how she appreciated his efforts to care for her. It was an act that was as natural as breathing to him. At the same time, while he enjoyed her thanks, he didn't need them. At least that's what he told himself.

"Call her," Abby said finally.

Jake

~~~

TAKING ABBY'S ADVICE, Jake stepped outside. He didn't want to make this call in front of Abby. It just didn't seem right.

The sun was high in the sky, taking the remaining chill in the air from the storm and warming it up. It wasn't too hot; you would still need a light jacket, but tomorrow would be bright and beautiful again. He paced on the deck a little while he worked up the nerve to dial Jen's number. After a few minutes, he decided it was now or never. The phone rang a few times, but no one answered. Jake was about to end the call when, finally, Jen picked up.

"Jake?" Jen's voice asked through the phone. She sounded like she had been crying.

"Are you crying? Jen, what's wrong?" Jake asked, alarm setting in. Abby was right. He wasn't a bad guy despite everything Jen had put him through. Despite the heartache and humiliation, Jake would never wish her ill.

"Can you talk? Is now a good time?" Jen asked, her voice shaking.

A deck chair that had been blown from somewhere on the island lay nearby. Jake walked over, picked it up, and took a seat.

"What's so urgent, Jen? You are starting to worry me," Jake said, his brow furrowed. His stomach twisted. His father always told him to trust his gut, and right then, his heart was telling him that his life was about to change.

Jen fell quiet. The distant sound of her sobbing told him she held the phone away from her face.

"Jen? Jen, talk to me," he insisted. Jake listened as Jen slowly returned to the phone, still sobbing; her pain tugged at him. He couldn't lie. He still cared for her, even if he didn't want to be with her.

"He found out, and he left me. I guess it's karma, really, after what I did to you," she began, her sobs getting harder and louder.

"Found out what, Jen?" Jake asked. He was starting to feel frustrated. She had left him several missed calls and texts saying how important it was that she speak with him, yet so far, she had given him no real answers.

"He said he wouldn't be a part of it if it weren't his, and based on the dates, I just don't know," she cried. Jake froze. His heart sounded loud in his ears; the rhythm was rapid as if he'd been running. He'd started putting two and two together and didn't like much how it was adding up.

"Jen, what are you saying?" he asked finally. He already knew the answer, or at least he thought he did, but he needed to hear it from the horse's mouth.

"I'm pregnant, and I don't know who the father is," she said, finally breaking down into uncontrollable sobs.

Jake was glad he was sitting down. He suddenly felt dizzy, like someone had pulled the rug out from under him. His mind was spinning. He couldn't believe what he was hearing. A baby. It was all he had ever wanted, but the circumstances were not ideal.

Abby

WHILE JAKE WENT OUTSIDE to call his ex, Abby took it upon herself to wash the dishes and clean up the kitchen. It was the least she could do to thank him for taking such good care of her. She looked out the window and could see him pacing, rubbing his hands over his face, visibly anxious. *I wonder what's happened. I hope he's okay*, she thought as she scrubbed the skillet.

Deciding it would be rude to eavesdrop, she finished her task and headed upstairs to shower and change. She was sticky from last night's fever, and a shower always cleared her mind.

After her shower, she dressed in one of her sports dresses and a light jacket. There was still a slight nip in the air even as the sun shone brightly from above. She headed for the widow's walk to assess the fallout from the storm. To her surprise, it was minimal. Sure, there were fallen trees and branches and overturned chairs here and there, but none of the buildings had sustained any visible damage.

The garden seemed to have been hit the worst. Some of the plants would need replanting. Some were past saving. Even though the island was not hers, she felt a responsibility to help restore it. It had been her home for the last week, after all. Scanning the area, she made a mental note of what she could do to help and headed back downstairs.

Abby stopped at the top of the stairs when she heard Jake's voice. She hadn't noticed he had come back inside. He was still on the phone. With nowhere else to go to get away from the conversation, she couldn't help but overhear.

"Do you think it's mine? But there is a chance it could be his?" Jake groaned. Abby took a step closer and heard the sound of Jake crashing down on the sofa.

"You know I want children, but yes, the situation isn't ideal. So what? Of course, I'll be there. How could you think I wouldn't? You are not alone, Jen."

Abby sat down on the top step; she felt for Jake. He was in an impossible situation. In the short time she had spent with him, she knew he was an honorable man, one in a million, really. But, unfortunately, men like Jake were hard to come by. Her stomach flipped. She had hoped she would have more time to get to know him. She liked what she had witnessed so far. But Abby wasn't prepared to get in the middle of something so messy. And given where this conversation was going, things were chaotic.

"When is your doctor's appointment? Okay, where is it? Great, I'll be there." Jake ended the call and fell silent. What was he thinking right now?

Abby couldn't hide any longer. She waited a little moment to give him some privacy before heading downstairs. He was slumped on the sofa, his head resting back, and his eyes closed. He looked stressed, and all Abby wanted to do was comfort him.

"Would you like a tea? Coffee?" she asked softly. Jake jumped, and Abby couldn't help but smile. "Sorry, I didn't mean to startle you," she said, leaning against the wall.

Jake sat forward and rested his head in his hands. Eventually, he sat up and said, "Coffee would be great, thank you."

Abby headed into the kitchen to make the coffee allowing Jake another moment alone with his thoughts. *Should I tell him I overheard? Should I ask about the call? No, it's none of my business.* Grabbing a pack of cookies from the shelf, she placed a few on a plate and took everything into the living room.

"Jen's pregnant." He blurted out the words, staring into his cup, watching the steam.

Abby nodded. "I heard. Sorry, I didn't mean to eavesdrop; it's a pretty small space," she said gently.

Jake didn't seem to mind that she had overheard. He proceeded to tell Abby the entire conversation about how Jen's Portuguese model lover had left because he wasn't sure the baby was his. Jake told her he knew it was just an excuse. The model had no interest in being a father.

Abby listened, gently nodding as Jake continued to tell her how Jen didn't know what she wanted to do and was scared. He planned to go with her to her next doctor's appointment.

"I'm sorry, I shouldn't be burdening you will all my issues," he said, finally meeting her gaze. The corner of his mouth slightly turned up as he continued, "I guess I just find it easy to talk to you."

Abby blushed, placing her cup on the table, and she did something she hadn't done since she was in school. She playfully tucked her hair behind her ear.

Am I flirting like a teenager? A woman of my age? How embarrassing, she felt her face flush, and she sat up straight as she realized what she needed to do.

"I will get out of your hair. I'll pack my things and have Bobbi take me back when she arrives. You don't need me in your way," she said, half rising with the intent of heading upstairs.

Jake lurched forward, taking her hand with a pained look on his face. He urged her to sit back down. Sitting next to him on the sofa, Abby waited patiently for him to continue. Her pulse raced as she hoped it would be good news.

"Don't go. My offer still stands. You shouldn't need to go. I will only be gone for a few days while I try and figure out what happens next with Jen, and then when I come back, we can discuss things further," he said.

Abby was intrigued. His response gave her hope, but she still didn't want to be a burden. Finally, taking a second to think things over, she nodded. Jake was right. She still had nowhere else to go. She could take a few days to enjoy the rest of her stay and look online to figure out what her next move should be.

Jake

JAKE NEEDED to clear his head. He couldn't seem to get his thoughts straight. He had planned on asking Abby to stay and eventually confessing to her that he was starting to have feelings for her. Still, he wanted the timing to be right. But, with Jen's bombshell, would the timing ever be right?

Rather than think about it, he turned his mind to other matters. Abby had suggested they spend the rest of the day cleaning up the island as best they could before he had to head to Portland. Jake thought it was a great idea. There's nothing like manual labor and getting your hands dirty to occupy the mind.

Abby tended to the garden, potting any plant that could be saved and gathering anything that couldn't be for the compost bin. Jake had tried to insist she get some more rest, but Abby refused, being the ever-strong and independent woman. The garden was a good compromise. It was an easy task that would not take up much of her energy.

Jake was happy to keep his distance while checking on the boat and mending the broken boards on the dock. As the day went by, they got through quite a bit of work. Once Abby had run out of gardening projects, she started picking up small branches and other debris from the lawn and walkways. She stayed within earshot but seemed to know he needed space.

A large tree had fallen on the path to the caretaker's cabin. Jake got the chainsaw and cut it into smaller logs, which he loaded into the tractor-trailer to be split and dried for firewood.

When he had unloaded the logs and started splitting them, he caught Abby staring at him from the window. It was getting hot, so he took off his shirt, determined to make it worth her while.

He lost track of time while he worked. How long she watched him, he didn't know. The day wore on, and finally, Jake had to stop to catch his breath. Sweat pooled at his brow, and his muscles ached. Maybe he'd overdone it. Pulling up a chair, he took a seat, grateful for the opportunity to sit down. He was looking out at the bay when he heard Abby approaching. She carried a small tray with a jug and two glasses.

"I thought you might be thirsty, so I made lemonade," she said, placing the tray on a nearby tree stump and pouring them both a glass. Jake downed the first glass in a single gulp. It was delicious, the perfect blend of bitter and sweet. She smiled and poured him another drink.

"Lunch will be ready soon if you're hungry," she said, looking out over the space he had cleared, letting the sun hit her face.

"I'm okay, thanks," he insisted, picking up his ax and getting ready to swing it at the last bit of the fallen tree trunk. Abby stepped forward, grabbing the ax and pulling it out of his grasp. Jake gawped at her. He had not expected her to do that and admired her strength. He had a pretty firm grip, and she quickly pulled it away from him.

"Jake. I know you are going through something right now, but you still need to take care of yourself. You haven't stopped all day. Come, eat," she insisted, turning and heading back to the main house, taking the ax with her.

Sweet, funny, and sassy. I could get used to this, he thought, then instantly shook the thought off.

After lunch, Jake went to Bobbi's cabin to pack the rest of his things. Once he'd cleaned up the place and changed the sheets, he sat on the bed. *What am I going to do?* He wanted to be a father more than anything in the world. But how would he navigate it with Jen? He never wanted to be a part-time dad. He never wanted to miss a thing. The thought of not being there when his child took its first steps or missing the first word made him physically ill. The thought tugged at his heart. He tried to convince himself that being there part-time was better than nothing, but he still wanted more. Would he move in with Jen? Would they try again? He had so many questions that they were giving him a headache.

Grabbing his things, he went to the dock to load the boat only to find Abby at the dock waiting for him.

"You didn't think you were leaving without saying goodbye, did you?"

She smiled. He smiled back, happy to see her.

"Of course not," he replied.

She nudged his arm playfully. "Yeah, yeah. Anyway, I decided to take you up on your offer and stay. I'll be here when you get back. Just take it easy. You have my number if you need a friend to talk to," she said.

"Ouch. Did you just put me in the friend zone?" he said out loud without thinking. He was mentally kicking himself as soon as the words fell from his lips. Abby let out a laugh. Happiness took over her face, her smile truly reaching her eyes for the first time since he'd met her. Jake decided he liked seeing her laugh.

"Isn't it better than being in the stranger zone?" she asked. She leaned in and kissed his cheek softly before heading back to the main house. He watched her walk away, mesmerized by the sway in her hips and the spring in her step.

Once Abby was back inside, he loaded his things into the boat and headed for the mainland. Next stop, Portland.

$\mathcal{J}$ en

⁓⊷

JEN SAT in the reception area of her OBGYN's office, picking nervously at her cuticles. Her manicurist would kill her. The receptionist had given her a leaflet about the first stages of pregnancy, but Jen wasn't ready to read it. She'd tossed it on the side table as she took in the other people in the waiting room. Women at various stages of pregnancy sat with their partners. She was the only one sitting alone.

She pulled out her phone and texted Jake demanding to know when he would be there. *He is going to be late,* she thought, bouncing her leg, annoyed at the sound of her high heel clicking on the marble floor. She wasn't the only one. She could see the irritated looks she was getting from the others in the room but didn't care.

Gasping for breath, Jake rushed through the door. Jen shot him a furious look. He hurried over and sat next to her.

"Sorry, traffic was terrible," he panted.

Jen rolled her eyes. Checking the clock above the reception desk, she saw he'd arrived with all of five minutes to spare.

"It's fine," she said, relaxing a little. She felt like she had been there for hours. *I can't wait to get out of here.*

Jake placed his hand on her knee, which instantly stopped bouncing. She glanced up at him and felt a little more at ease. His eyes were so gentle and full of love and care that they warmed her. She remembered the reasons why she'd dated him in the first place.

"Your nervous, I get it. But I'm here now. You're not alone," Jake said, putting his arm around her and gently kissing her on the forehead. The gesture unsettled her further. She didn't want him kissing her, but at the same time, she liked the sudden contact.

"Thanks," she smiled up at him, hoping he didn't notice the way her lips trembled.

The nurse called her name just then, and Jen found she couldn't bring herself to stand up. She sat shaking until she felt the comforting pressure of Jake's hand on her shoulder.

"I'm right here," he whispered.

Summoning whatever courage she could find, Jen stood and walked through the double doors and down the corridor, trying to ignore all the pregnant women. Dimly, she was aware of big protruding bellies and women waddling side to side in discomfort. *I don't want this; I don't want any of this.* The panicked thoughts circled relentlessly, making her ill.

"So, I can see here we are confirming the pregnancy, is that right?" asked the doctor as she looked over Jen's file.

Jen nodded her reply, afraid to say the words aloud. Saying it out loud made it real. A nurse gave her a gown and a clear plastic container for a urine sample and pointed Jen toward the door. Once she was inside the bathroom, she began to hyperventilate. Panicking that she couldn't breathe only made her panic more. She clung to the sink while staring at her reflection, trying to calm her breathing. The nurse knocked on the door to check on her, and it made her jump.

"I'll be right out," she said, giving herself a pep talk before getting the sample the doctor had requested.

In the exam room with Jake, Jen was very self-conscious in her hospital gown. The nurse took her blood pressure, then a blood sample. "We'll have the results shortly," she said, leaving Jake and Jen alone. Jen looked around at all the medical equipment and pictures of smiling babies on the walls, forcing herself to push back the tears brimming her eyes.

"This is a nightmare," she whispered.

"What? Did you say something?" Jake asked, glancing up from a pamphlet on pregnancy he'd picked up from the display of leaflets next to the door.

"What? No, nothing. It's fine," Jen stammered, bouncing her leg and fidgeting with her gown.

"You're such a bad liar. You always bounce your leg when you're nervous, and you haven't stopped since I got here," Jake said, giving her a sympathetic look. She opened her mouth to speak, but the doctor came in. She pulled the privacy curtain and nodded her head at Jake to wait in her office when Jen said she'd rather he wasn't there for the exam.

Alone with Jen, the doctor had her scoot to lie down, scoot up, and then put her feet in the stirrups. "It's just a routine pelvic exam. The blood and urine tests will tell us if you're pregnant or not, but the exam will give us a little more information."

Jen nodded and made a non-committal sound while she tried to relax. When the doctor was done, she pulled off her gloves and told Jen she could get dressed and join them next door when she was ready.

Once she was alone, Jen sat up and swung her feet to the side of the table. She took deep breaths, bracing herself for the news ahead. Eventually, she got up, dressed, and joined Jake and the doctor in the room next door.

She sat down and looked at Jake. He gave her his patient smile, and she tried to smile back, though she was sure she looked like a strangled cat. She faced the doctor expectantly.

"Congratulations, you're pregnant," the doctor said, tapping a few keys at her computer and turning the monitor so they both could see the results for themselves. "According to the HCG levels and the date of your last cycle, we think about six weeks. But there is only one way to know for sure. Can you pop up on the table for me, and we will get to see your baby," the doctor explained, motioning her over to where a table covered in tissue waited, ready for use.

Jen looked at Jake out of the corner of her eye. The joy that lit up his face made her palms sweat. *I'm going to have to break his heart,* she thought, tears brimming her eyes. *Pull yourself together Jen, all first-time mothers feel scared. You might feel different when you see the baby,* she argued with herself, finally turning her head to the screen. The doctor poured the gold jello on her belly and gently maneuvered the wand. After a few seconds, the visible signs of a baby popped up on the screen. A tiny pulsing caught Jen's eye, and the doctor flicked a switch. The tiny heartbeat reminded Jen of a hummingbird as it echoed in the room.

"Based on the size, I would say you are between nine and ten weeks," the doctor chirped. Jen lay watching the screen, hoping she would feel something, anything other than the gut-wrenching fear she had felt all day.

"Wow, it's real," Jake said. Jen looked over, and tears rolled down her face. Jake was so happy, happier than she had ever seen him.

Jake

~~∿~~

JAKE COULDN'T PULL his eyes away from the sonogram. The moment he saw that tiny beating heart, his entire body was filled with a feeling he had never felt before. Joy, love, and electricity filled his veins, a pull so natural and paternal linked him to the tiny image on the screen. Unconditional love. *My baby*, he thought. His chest felt so tight that he thought his heart might burst. Nothing on earth could compare to that feeling.

As they left the doctor's office, Jake could hear Jen talking, but he wasn't listening. When he saw her storm off ahead, he jogged over to keep pace with her.

"Jen, what's wrong?" he asked, stopping in front of her and forcing her to stop and look at him. He had been so busy thinking about how happy he was that he didn't consider how she felt. Her eyes were puffy and red. Even her mascara ran down her cheeks.

"I can't do this, Jake. I'm sorry, I can't," she sobbed, wrapping her arms around herself. Jake couldn't tell if it was to keep warm or as an act of defense. She refused to meet his gaze.

"That's natural. All first-time moms get the jitters," he said, placing a hand on her shoulder. "As I said, you're not alone," he continued, hoping to comfort her. But her head snapped up, and the pain in her eyes was replaced with fury; her face scrunched in anger. She pushed Jake's hand off her shoulder.

"You don't get it, Jake. I don't want you. I don't want any of this. I appreciate that you want to help, but I don't want this life. I don't want sleepless nights and dirty diapers," she yelled, getting more flustered with every word. "Do you know what I saw in that sonogram room? The end of my life. At first, I thought it was just jitters, but when I looked at that screen, I felt nothing." Her whole body shook with her sobs. "Some people are not meant to be parents," she said softly as her voice caught and fresh tears began to fall. Jake tried to step in to comfort her, but she pulled back.

"No, Jake, don't touch me," she yelled.

Jake stared at her, lost. He didn't know what to do. Panic began to set in. "Okay, just tell me what I can do," he said finally.

Jen shook her head, looking to the sky for help before looking Jake dead in the eye and dropping another bombshell.

"I don't want this baby. I want an abortion." She spoke without flinching.

Abby

ABBY SPENT the next day fixing the last few patches of the garden and decided to take advantage of being on the island alone as the weather had picked up. Feeling incredibly daring, she stripped out of her bikini, and she dove into the watering hole for a swim. The water was cool on her skin, but she welcomed it as it was a scorching day. The storm had cleared the air beautifully, and the sun shone brighter and hotter in the sky. Abby was glad Jake had offered her to stay, and she was even happier she accepted. She had grown quite fond of her little tropical paradise and found that the longer she stayed, the less she wanted to leave.

After her swim, she sunbathed naked on a soft beach towel, hoping to even out her tan lines after playing some music on her phone. Feeling more content than she had in a long time, she pressed play and soaked up the sun's rays, enjoying the vitamin D as she sank back into her happy place.

Later that night, as she ate dinner watching a romantic comedy on Netflix on her laptop, she realized she hadn't heard from Jake. Even though she barely knew him, she worried about him. He had seemed stressed when he left. His words from the previous morning repeated over and over in her mind. "When I come back, we can discuss things further." She fantasized about what that could mean and found she hoped to deepen their friendship. As if on cue, her phone rang, and Jake's name flashed on her screen.

"Hi Jake, how are you?" she asked, pressing pause so she didn't miss any of the movie.

"I'm...well, not great if I'm honest," he answered.

Abby's heart sank; she didn't like hearing Jake so upset. "What's wrong? What happened?" she asked.

Jake sighed as though the weight of the world rested upon his shoulders. "She's nine weeks pregnant—" he began.

Abby interrupted without thinking. "That's wonderful news. Congratulations!"

A moment later, reality set in. She realized that the possibility of him coming back for her was slim. He had been engaged to Jen, they were getting married, and now they were due to have a baby. Abby knew Jake was the type of man to stand by the women he got pregnant with and imagined them restarting their relationship. *So, where does that leave me?* she thought. *This is precisely the kind of mess I didn't want to get sucked into.*

"She wants an abortion," Jake said plainly, breaking into her thoughts. Abby could hear the pain in his voice.

"Oh," was all she could manage. She loved her kids and could never imagine giving them up, but she knew not all women thought like her. Ultimately, it *was* Jen's decision. "I don't know what to say, Jake. I'm sorry." She got up and slowly paced around the room.

"I've asked her for a paternity test. I've told her if the baby is mine and she still decided she doesn't want to keep it, I will take it and give it the best life," he continued with such joy and enthusiasm. Abby couldn't help but smile; she knew how much Jake wanted to be a father, and she did not doubt in her mind that he would be a great dad.

"And what did she say?" Abby asked. Jake fell silent for so long that Abby wondered if she had lost cell service.

"She said she will think about it. I'm going to stay here for a few more days and keep an eye on her. Hopefully, once she has had a few days to think things over and let the news sink in, she can look at it with fresh eyes," he answered.

His voice sounded tired, but something else was going on. Abby could tell he was still unsure about something. He was hesitating. "Jake, what's on your mind? I can practically see the worry lines on your face."

"I mean, I can't force her to have the baby at the end of the day. It's her body. She has to carry the baby and then give birth. I don't want to force the issue," he sighed again. And again, the pause felt like something was missing from what he was saying.

"...but?" Abby asked, prodding him a little, hoping to get to the heart of the matter.

"But, god Abby, I have wanted to be a father for as long as I can remember, and now I have my chance. I can't describe how amazing it felt seeing that sonogram and hearing the heartbeat. It's just...It was..."

"Magical?" Abby answered, finishing his sentence. But, of course, she knew. Nothing beats that feeling. It is a memory that Abby treasured and would keep with her, fresh in her memory, for the rest of her life.

"Exactly, I'll never forget it," he said, and Abby could hear the smile on his face, but his happiness was short-lived as doubt crept back into his voice.

"God, Abby, what if it's not mine? What if it is, but she decides to abort anyway? I don't think I can handle this," he said. Abby was shocked at his honesty but was glad he felt he could confide in her.

"Give it a few days. Allow her the space to process everything. Take it one day at a time, and Jake. As hard as it is, please try not to get your hopes up. Prepare for the worst but hope for the best," she said.

They talked for a bit longer. Primarily small talk: Jake's drive to Portland, what they ate for dinner, how Abby was feeling, and her activities for the day. Finally, she ended the call by informing Jake that she planned to start writing her mystery novel in the coming days and told him to keep in touch.

When Abby went to bed that night, all she could think about was Jake. *She knew it would break his heart if Jen chose to abort or the baby wasn't his.* The idea of him having to go through that hurt Abby, and a stray tear left her eye as she fell asleep.

Jake

JAKE SPENT the next few days leaving Jen to her thoughts and catching up on some work. He needed something to distract him. He had hardly eaten in days, and sleep didn't come easy. The only thing keeping him sane was his daily texts with Abby. She had proven to be a godsend. He didn't want to burden her with all his worries, but she was so easy to talk to. Their conversations often led to discussions about the baby.

He was pleased that the situation hadn't scared her away. She seemed pretty content on the island alone. Bobbi was due to join her in a day or two. Jake had called Bobbi briefly, informing her about the situation. He made the mistake of checking the local news sites and found that someone had reported Jen's pregnancy. He couldn't figure out who had found out. He assumed someone at the doctor's office had put two and two together and thought the news might be a nice payday. Thankfully, Jen's publicist denied the entire thing, but the rumors had already begun. *Great, just what I need*, he thought, pouring himself a small glass of brandy. He wasn't usually a drinker but found one a night was the sweet spot to help him drift off to sleep. Jen had agreed to Jake staying in her spare room while she thought things over. Initially, he insisted on going home but had decided to stay after some thought.

Jake had been with Jen for four days, each day biting his tongue. Jen needed to decide independently, and he didn't want to pressure her or stress her out. Stress wasn't good for the baby. He sat at her dining table reading and eating granola when Jen sat down with him.

"I've come to a decision," she said. The look on her face told Jake it wasn't good news. He sat back and braced himself for the worst.

"I can't go through with the paternity test. It wouldn't be fair. I'm sorry, Jake, I can't have this baby," she told him. Jake could tell she wasn't trying to hurt him, but he couldn't help feeling his heart shatter into a million pieces. His dream was in his grasp, and now it was slipping away; he was losing it. A part of him wished she hadn't told him in the first place.

"Is it the birth that worries you?" he asked.

Jen paused, thinking through her answer. "Maybe...honestly, I don't know. It's complicated. I can't explain it," she said. She was visibly uncomfortable justifying her answer, and Jake felt terrible for pushing. Still, he had questions of his own he needed answering. As Jen went to leave, he grabbed her hand, his eyes pleading with her to listen.

"I'm not going to force you to change your mind, but please, at least do the paternity test. I need to know if it's mine," Jake pleaded.

Jen rolled her eyes and pulled her hand away. "Why Jake? What is it going to prove? If it is yours, it changes nothing. I still don't want to have the baby. If it's not yours, you will be heartbroken. Either way, it ends badly. I told you because I was scared and didn't know what to do. But now, I have had time to make up my mind. I wish I hadn't brought you into this. I feel awful. I've hurt you enough. I don't want to hurt you again," she said, turning to leave.

Jake couldn't help himself; he needed to fight his case. "Well, you did tell me, and you're right. Either way, I'm the one getting hurt again. At least give me the courtesy of the paternity test because not knowing is driving me insane. At least if I know, either way, I will know how to deal with it," he said, jumping to his feet a little more forcibly than he intended.

Jen slowly turned back. She looked him over before sighing profoundly and reluctantly agreeing to the test.

"Thank you, I know I am asking a lot of you, and I want you to know I appreciate it," Jake said.

Jen rolled her eyes and stalked off to her room.

A few days later, they traveled to the doctor's office together. No matter how many times Jake tried to talk to Jen, she ignored him. He knew he had crossed a line and kicked himself for it. Jen had agreed to an uncomfortable, invasive test that had risks out of guilt. *What am I doing? This is wrong,* he thought, stopping the car and pulling over.

Jen looked over, alarmed.

"Do you want to go through with this? If you say no, I won't force you. Don't do this just for me," he said, needing her to understand he meant these words with every fiber of his being.

"No, I want to do it. I thought about it, and I need to know too," she answered, and they continued their journey.

After the test, the doctor informed them the results would be ready in four days.

Abby

ABBY WOKE, and the first thing she did was check her phone. She had a few messages from her kids checking in, but the one she wanted most was the text from Jake. Though their time together had been cut short, they had continued to flirt via text and phone calls. Abby found she looked forward to her good morning text from Jake more and more. But that morning, there was no news from Jake. She replied to her kids and tried to ignore the slight disappointment that rose in her.

After showering and dressing, she took her coffee up to the widow's walk. The view was stunning as usual. She noticed a few dark clouds on the horizon and suspected rainfall. But while the sun still shone overhead, she decided to explore the rest of the island. So, after breakfast, she grabbed her hiking boots and a bottle of water and headed out.

With her headphones on, she happily walked trail after trail. Bobbi was due to arrive soon, and she looked forward to meeting her. Jake had told Abby lots about Bobbi, and she seemed like the type of person Abby would get along well with. While she enjoyed her solitude, she looked forward to having someone else on the island with her.

As she reached Bobbi's cabin, she felt a few drops of rain. It wasn't too heavy, and the air was still warm, so she didn't rush back until the rain started to fall heavily. She sprinted back to the main house, laughing to herself when she arrived at the door. After drying out, she made lunch and settled by a window watching the rain, enjoying the sound of it tapping on the roof.

"Well, now is as good a time as any," she said, gathering her laptop and settling in to start her novel. She and Jake had spoken about it so much as of late that she found she was full of excitement and enthusiasm and couldn't wait to get started. She made notes about her characters and all her ideas for the plot. Planning it out only got her more excited. *This is real. I'm actually going to do this.* She took a picture and sent it to Jake.

He texted back instantly.

Great job. I can't wait to read it.

Hours passed, and Abby's stomach began to rumble. She had been so engrossed in her task that she hadn't noticed the rain stop. Looking at the time, she decided dinner was in the cards. Checking her phone, she was disappointed to see no further messages from Jake. "What are you doing? You're acting like a child, woman up," she said to herself as she got up and headed to the kitchen. She liked Jake but couldn't figure out why he was breaking down all her defenses and making her act like a woman years her junior so easily. "He has a lot on his plate. Leave him be. He will be in touch when he has time," she said to the empty room as she started dinner.

Halfway through preparing dinner, Abby heard a knock on the door. Freezing, she stood unsure of what to do. She was on an island alone. *Who could it be?* The knock sounded again, and Abby decided to be brave and open the door. A tall woman with angular features and hair tied tight in a bun stood at the door.

"Abby? Hi, I'm Bobbi," she said, holding out her hand for a handshake. Abby burst out laughing. Bobbi slowly pulled back her hand and looked back in confusion.

"I'm sorry, I completely forgot you were arriving today, and I had a little freaked out when you knocked on the door. Come in, come in," Abby said, composing herself with a quick smile.

Bobbi gave a slight grin at the statement. "I can see why you would be scared. You have been on an island alone for a few days. So, it's understandable."

"How can I help?" Abby asked, heading back into the kitchen to finish dinner.

"I came to introduce myself and let you know I'm here if you need anything," Bobbi said, looking around the room. She stopped when her eyes fell on the books on the chair by the fireplace.

"Oh, sorry, Jake, let me borrow them. I hope you don't mind. You can take them if you like. I have finished them," Abby said quickly. Bobbi didn't seem to mind, but Abby worried. She wouldn't like it herself if someone borrowed her things when she wasn't home.

Bobbi only smiled as she picked up the books.

"Would you like to stay for dinner? I should be finished with it shortly," Abby asked and was thankful when Bobbi accepted.

They sat enjoying the chicken and vegetables Abby had prepared and enjoyed a glass of wine, each talking about books and their favorite things about the island. Bobbi seemed cagey at first. She was the epitome of professionalism. Abby was happy that Bobbi felt she could relax and be herself around her. After dinner, Abby headed into the kitchen to put the dishes in to soak. She planned on washing them once Bobbi had left.

When Abby came back into the living room, she panicked, seeing Bobbi glancing over what she had written so far. She ran over and slammed the laptop shut.

"Sorry, I didn't mean to intrude. It's good." Bobbi smiled self-consciously.

Abby smiled back, though the gesture was automatic and slightly forced. "Thanks, it's just a first draft," she said, scooping up her laptop and popping it aside.

"You have talent, stick with it," Bobbi encouraged.

Abby relaxed when she realized the other woman had enjoyed her writing but needed a subject change, so she asked the question she had wanted to ask since Bobbi arrived. "Have you spoken with Jake? How is he?"

Bobbi clammed up, looking hesitant to say anything about her boss.

"It's okay. I know what's happened. I haven't spoken to him today and was getting a little worried. It can't be easy, what he's going through," Abby said, hoping to encourage Bobbi to answer.

Finally, after a moment, Bobbi answered, "He's okay. He's just waiting on the paternity results. Any day now."

They made small talk for a little longer before Bobbi gathered her things and left after thanking Abby for a lovely dinner. Finally, alone Abby let worry and doubt set into her mind. *What if he has stopped calling because they have discussed getting back together if the baby is his?*

Abby kicked herself for allowing herself to feel for him. She cursed herself for getting involved in the situation in the first place. Finally, after she cleaned up the dishes and put them away, she had time to calm her mind. She decided to give Jake the benefit of the doubt. *He is going through so much. Give him the time. He will call,* she thought before finally retiring for the evening.

Jake

JAKE WALKED into the kitchen to make himself something to eat. His stomach growled loudly. He had hardly eaten since he arrived in Portland, and his appetite was starting to come back. He was famished. But, as he turned the corner, he froze. Sitting at the dining table just past the kitchen island were Jen and the Portuguese model, Francisco Silva.

Jake's brows furrowed deep; his blood began to boil. *Motherfucker has some nerve*, Jake thought, slowly walking towards them. Jen held an envelope in her hands, and her knee bounced under the table.

"What are you doing here? I heard you ran off," he snarled, folding his arms and refusing to sit with them at the table.

"Jake, please, this is hard enough," Jen pleaded.

He felt for her. He wasn't angry at her. He was mad at Silva. His sudden arrival couldn't mean anything good.

"Please sit," Jen said, pointing the envelope at the chair opposite Silva. Hesitantly, Jake sat down, his gaze burning toward Silva. Silva sat back in his chair casually with his sunglasses still on, even inside the house.

"Why are you here?" Jake asked across the table.

"I have had time to think, and I overreacted. There is a chance the baby is mine, and I want to know for sure," Silva answered.

96

The fact that Silva thought that the baby could be his confirmed Jake's suspicions that Jen decided to leave even before the wedding. The confirmation infuriated him more. But the baby was more important.

"Is that the results?" Jake asked, pointing to the envelope.

Jen nodded, "I can't open it," she said.

Jake went to take the envelope from her gently, but Silva snatched it from her hands. "Hey!" Jake yelled. But Silva tore open the envelope, taking off his sunglasses; his eyes scanned over the document. Jen and Jake stared at him, both filled with anxiety, waiting for the answer to the question they all were asking.

"Who is the father?" Jake finally asked.

Silva slammed the letter on the table, and a slow grin crept up his face. "The baby is mine," he said, leaping up and pulling Jen from her seat, spinning her around in excitement. "I'm going to be a daddy," he cheered.

Jake looked over at Jen, who looked back with apologetic eyes. He snatched the letter; he needed to read the results for himself. *I'm not the father,* he thought, tossing the letter to the floor. He stormed out, slamming the door behind him.

He paced streets with no real direction. He was filled with anger, pain, and energy. He needed to walk until he didn't feel anymore. Over the last few days, he had thought he had made peace with the situation. Instead, he had done nothing but think about the possibility that the baby wasn't his. But deep down, he couldn't deny that he had hoped the baby was his all along. He had hoped he could convince Jen to carry the baby to term. He had hoped she would change her mind. He tried to prepare for what he had thought was the worst, but nothing could prepare him for the gut-wrenching pain he felt when he'd read the results.

He walked downtown until he reached a walkway overlooking the Willamette River and stopped just looking out over the river at the city on the other side. The sounds of a baby crying nearby made him turn his head. A young couple out on a stroll stopped and sat on a bench to feed their baby. All the emotions Jake had been holding in came flooding to the surface, and he cried; tears rolled down his face, and his chest ached for the baby he had gained and lost in less than a week.

He stayed at the waterfront sobbing until the sun had set, and he felt like there were no tears left. His eyes ached, and the flesh around them felt puffy. He headed back to Jen's apartment and packed his things. He wanted nothing more than to go home. He needed to be alone. As he grabbed his things and headed to the door, Jen cut him off at the front door blocking him from leaving.

"You've been crying!" Jen said in surprise.

"What do you want, Jen?" he asked, trying not to look at her.

"I wanted you to hear it from me before you read it in the tabloids," she began. Her words caught Jake's attention, and he finally looked at her. Her gaze was cast to the floor as though she couldn't bear to look at him when she delivered yet another blow.

"Francisco and I are keeping the baby. We are going to raise it together," she said, her tone barely audible.

Jake thought he had misheard. "Sorry I didn't quite catch that," he said, trying not to lose his temper again.

"I'm keeping the baby," she said again.

Jake felt the fire rise in his veins again. "So, what you're telling me is you didn't want the baby when there was a possibility it was mine? It wasn't the baby you had issues with. It was me?"

It wasn't really a question. Maybe that was just as well, considering Jen didn't answer. Instead, she kept her eyes cast to the floor, avoiding his gaze.

"Move out of my way, Jen," he said briskly. This time when he left, he didn't look back. Jen called after him, but he didn't listen. He was done with Jen for good.

Abby

ABBY TRIED TO CALL JAKE, but he never answered and ignored her texts. She was worried about him; he hadn't had a problem talking with her before. She tried distracting herself by writing the rest of her novel, but her mind kept floating back to Jake. She asked Bobbi, and she hadn't heard from him since her arrival either. Abby thought the worst.

"He obviously found out he is the father and is staying in Portland with Jen," she mumbled as she hiked around the island. A long walk usually cleared her head, but today it just fueled her thoughts. "Why did I allow myself to fall for him? What did I think was going to happen?" she mumbled as she walked around the Annex heading back toward the main house.

When she arrived, Bobbi was waiting at the door. Abby saw the other woman was frowning and jogged over.

"Hi Bobbi, what's up?" she asked, opening the door, and allowing them both inside.

"Have you heard from Jake? I have tried to contact him about a few repairs, but he isn't responding." Bobbi's face was pale, her expression serious.

Abby shook her head but tried to stay positive. "I haven't, but I'm sure he will be fine. He probably just wants some time alone," she said, acting as if she wasn't being eaten alive by her own racing thoughts.

Bobbi nodded. "If you hear from him, will you let me know? I'll do the same," she said before leaving Abby alone.

Three more days passed with no word from Jake. Abby was starting to become annoyed. She felt ignored and rejected. If he wasn't interested, all he had to do was say so. The longer she didn't hear from him, the more she felt like a burden. *What if he decides not to come back? I can't stay here indefinitely,* she thought. She scanned the internet for places she could rent until she found something permanent. *It would be rude to leave without a word.* She tried to call Jake to discuss her stay with this thought in mind. To Abby's surprise, he answered the phone.

"Jake? How are you? I was beginning to worry," she said the moment he answered.

"I'm fine, just want to be alone for a while," he slurred.

He sounded like he had been drinking, and Abby's concern grew. "Are you drunk? Are you sure you don't want to talk?"

"Leave me alooooone, Abby."

The line went dead. *Just how drunk is he?*

Abby was furious. How dare he talk to her like that. She was only concerned about him, and he had dismissed her without a second thought. Staying had been a mistake. She made up her mind and packed her things. She ran up to Bobbi's cabin and knocked on the door. Bobbi opened the door looking like she had just received bad news.

"I guess you heard," Bobbi said, stepping aside and allowing Abby room to come in.

"Heard what?" Abby asked, trying not to let it show on her face how much it irritated her that Jake had clearly found it was okay speaking with Bobbi, though not with her. This vexed Abby more.

Bobbi sighed, handing Abby her phone. Loaded on the screen was an article from TMZ. It told the story of Jake and Jen being seen at the doctor's office together. It then went on to say there had been rumors of a paternity test. Abby read on; the article ended with Jen and her boyfriend Francisco Silva announcing they were having a baby.

"Oh no, Jake must be crushed," Abby said, handing back Bobbi's phone slowly while she struggled to think about what to do next.

In the end, the article cemented Abby's decision in her mind. She couldn't stay on the island any longer. Jake needed space. She wasn't prepared to burden him any longer. She told Bobbi of her plan to leave and asked for her help. She had called her realtor and had arranged to rent a cabin in Bar Harbour. She could figure out what to do from there.

On the boat ride off the island, Abby wiped a stray tear from her cheek. It wasn't a tear of sadness, more of frustration. She was angry with herself for falling for Jake. She hadn't gone to the island hoping to find someone. And, for a second, she had let down her guard. She couldn't take being hurt again. Leaving was the best thing for her.

Jake

ABBY, Trent, and Bobbi had called and texted multiple times, but Jake just wanted to be alone. He couldn't understand Jen's choices. He wasn't angry at her anymore, but he constantly asked himself what was wrong with him and why he hadn't been enough for her. Beating himself up only made things worse, and that's when he turned to drink. He never intended to drink his sorrows away, but it was easier than dealing with the pain.

The worst day was when Jen and Silva announced to the world that they were raising the baby together. TMZ and other tabloids and gossip rags had made several attempts to contact him for comment. The hotel was good about preserving his privacy. But on the one day he decided to swim laps in the pool, he found a paparazzi trying to climb over the garden wall. Jake hadn't realized the paparazzi had a buddy at the hotel, and when an article came out labeling him a sad drunk, he knew he had to get his act together.

He cleaned himself up, shaved – he hadn't shaved in a week – and spent a day in the gym working off what pent-up energy he had left. He called his employee hotline again and asked to speak to Melanie, the nice lady who had made him feel so much better the last time he called. He didn't need advice; he needed someone to listen. He could have called Abby; they were "friends." But the detached anonymity of a patient listener did wonders. Finally, he called Trent, letting his friend know he was okay. After a long conversation, Trent let him know he was always there for him and reassured Jake that he had things at the office well in hand.

He called Bobbi but got no answer. Assuming the cell service on the island was down again, he emailed her about the repairs she asked about and told her he would be back in a day or two.

Finally, he called Abby. He needed to apologize. He had spoken to her terribly when she had been nothing but pleasant to him, and he felt awful. He tried calling but got no response. Deciding he didn't want to apologize over text, that it had to be in person, he packed a bag and headed back to the island. He texted Bobbi his ETA so she could pick him up at the dock.

When the boat arrived, Bobbi waved at him. He boarded the boat and stashed his bag.

"Jake, it's so good to see you," she said with a smile.

"It's good to be back. Sorry I've been so distant. I was going through something, but thankfully I'm back now," he said, shaking her outstretched hand. Bobbi nodded toward the cockpit, and Jake shook his head. He'd been driving for hours; Bobbi could captain the boat back to Cherry Tree Island.

They didn't talk on the way. The engine was too noisy, and the bay was choppy. When they docked and headed to the main house, Jake took in the island. He was happy to see it returned to its former glory despite the storm. Bobbi and Abby had done a great job.

"Yes, sorry. I saw the TMZ reports. That must have been awful. But I'm glad to see you are doing better," she said. They stood in front of the main house and talked about the repairs and preparations for the next storm.

Jake placed an affectionate hand on Bobbi's shoulder. "Thanks for everything, Bobbi."

He nodded to the house. "Is Abby okay? I tried calling and texting her, but she didn't answer," he said.

Bobbi's face blanched. Jake's heart began to race when she didn't answer right away. He thought the worst. "Tell me Abby isn't hurt," he said finally.

"No, she's fine. But Jake, I... She's gone," Bobbi said and looked away.

Jake

JAKE PACED AROUND the main house, unable to concentrate on anything. Abby had left, and it was all his fault. He'd had a shot with a good woman, a phenomenal woman, and he had been too busy wallowing in self-pity to appreciate her.

She had kept in touch and been his sounding board. She had encouraged and supported him, even when it had looked like he was going to have to stay with Jen. Through it all, Abby was there.

Miserable, he slumped on the sofa, leaning forward, running his hands roughly over his face. As he straightened, he spotted something under the table. He picked it up and realized it was a page of Abby's notes for her novel.

He didn't read it, just admired her beautiful cursive handwriting and the odd doodle she had done in the corner of the page. He folded it neatly, put it in his pocket, and headed back to Bobbi's cabin.

He knocked on the door, and Bobbi promptly answered. Jake didn't give Bobbi a chance to say anything before he blurted out why he was there. "Where is she? I need to talk to her. She's ignoring my calls. Did she say where she was headed?" Jake asked, feeling more desperate than he'd ever felt.

Bobbi stood, her face a study of professionalism, expression unchanged. "I'm sorry, sir, I can't tell you that," she said.

"What? Why not?" Jake asked, a little angry that Bobbi wasn't willing to help.

"She asked me not to. I'm sorry. I know you're my employer, but I can't break that trust. I wouldn't break your trust, so I can't break hers," Bobbi said, her tone cool and reserved. Jake could tell from her eyes she wanted to tell him. And the fact she cared so much for Abby told Jake that Bobbi liked Abby. Jake trusted Bobbi's opinion a lot. Bobbi's opinion of Abby only made Jake more determined to find her.

"I understand." He sighed, running his hand through his hair.

"I don't know what to do, Bobbi." His voice caught, and he cleared his throat, trying to hide his emotions. Jake didn't have an issue showing or stating his feelings, but he still didn't like looking vulnerable.

"If you were Abby, where would you go?" Bobbi asked with a wink.

Jake looked back at Bobbi with confusion before he had his light bulb moment. He smiled and pointed at Bobbi, who chuckled as Jake raced back to the main house.

Jake knew Abby didn't have anywhere to go, and he didn't think she would have found permanent accommodations so soon. She had left not long before he arrived, so he knew she couldn't have gotten too far.

Back at the main house, he searched for places to rent within a small radius of the island. He found a few he thought Abby would like – and could afford based on how much she was willing to put down to move to the island. "Time to make some calls," he said, half under his breath, feeling the first stirrings of excitement now that he was on the trail.

He dialed the realtor who arranged for Abby to stay at the island in the first place and hoped she could at least point him in the right direction. The phone rang three times before she picked up.

"Hello Jake, how are you?" she asked, a smile in her voice.

"I'm very good, thank you. I wondered if you could help me. I'm trying to track down Abby. You know, the lady who made an offer on Cherry Tee Island?" he began.

There was a momentary silence before the agent spoke again. "Yes, but I'm sorry I can't help you. The privacy and security of our clients are of the utmost importance to us. It would be unethical for me to reveal any information on her whereabouts," she said, her voice ultra-professional. Jake could tell her boss was within earshot.

"Okay, then can you tell me which areas have been most popular for short-term rentals lately? I can give you a few places I think might be a good fit," Jake said, crossing his fingers, hoping she would and could help.

"What areas are you looking at? And I can see what we have available," she said, her tone flat.

Jake almost cheered. He had dealt with her for years on other properties, and they had a level of trust. He knew she was trying not to break the rules in front of her boss but would also tell him where Abby was. He listed the first two properties he'd found on his search only to receive a very generic response.

"Oh yes, that's a great area, plenty of property available," she answered. Her answer told Jake that no one had moved in recently, which ruled them out. Abby wasn't there.

"Okay, what about Bar Harbor? Anything there?" he asked.

"No, I'm afraid we rented the last cabin there a couple of days ago," she began. *Bingo, Abby's in Bar Harbor*, he thought.

"We have a few properties to rent on your first choice," she continued.

"How many?" he asked, understanding the secret code and what she said. She coughed lightly, and Jake could have sworn she said the word, "Cabin."

"Four," she answered.

He arranged to rent a cabin for a few days in hopes he could convince Abby he was worth a second chance. Once the rental deal was done, he sighed contently.

"Thank you," he ended the call, swiveling in his desk chair to give a triumphant fist pump.

"Cabin four, Abby, I'm on my way," he said to the empty house, the house that still had a subtle scent of Abby in the air. Filled with adrenaline and newfound hope, Jake grabbed his jacket and headed out straight away. Time was of the essence. Abby might decide to up and leave at any minute. He couldn't waste a second.

It was still early in the day, not quite noon, and the sun was high in the sky, bathing the area in hues of gold and warmth. It gave Jake a spring in his step. He told Bobbi where he was headed, and she greeted him with a smile.

"Go get her, sir," she winked and waved as Jake sped off to leave the island. Love awaited in Bar Harbor.

On his arrival, Jake headed to a local flower shop and grabbed a small bouquet of white and pink roses with a subtle mix of white blossoms and tulips. It was an odd combination, but he hoped Abby would like it.

He stood outside cabin four, listening to the low rumble of sounds from within. He knew she was home but still felt he needed a minute or two to pluck up the courage to speak. After a moment of silent reflection and going over his monologue in his mind, he tapped on the door. His heart started to race and the seconds it took Abby to open the door felt like hours.

She stood in front of him, her smile fading but her eyes still glowing at the sight of him. Neither said a word. Abby's eyes drifted to the bouquet Jake was clinging to like his life depended on it.

"Are those for me?" she asked, a faint smile lifting the corner of her lips.

Jake thrust the flowers to her and nodded, mentally kicking himself for falling apart in front of her. He couldn't seem to form the words that screamed in his mind.

Abby gently took the flowers from him and pulled them to her nose, her eyes closing as she inhaled the beautiful floral scent.

"How did you find me?" she asked, not looking up from the flowers.

"I had to see you. I needed to talk to you," he began, freezing as her eyes drifted back to his. He dove his hand into his back pocket and retrieved the notes she had left behind. "I found this at the house. I thought it might be important and wanted to return it to you." He smiled affably, finding confidence in being able to offer her something he knew she needed.

"Is that the only reason you are here?" she asked, placing the flowers on the small table just inside the door. They still stood on the doorstep. Jake could feel Abby's apprehension, and it pulled at his gut.

"May I come in?" he finally asked.

After a moment of silent reflection, she stepped aside and allowed Jake inside. "Why don't you sit down. I'll make some coffee." Abby snagged the flowers and headed to the small kitchenette to make a pot of coffee while Jake sat at the small, wooden dining table just the right size for two.

"I need to tell you how sorry I am for how I acted recently. It was very out of character for me, and you had been nothing but lovely and supportive. Abby, you need to know how truly sorry I am if I have hurt you," Jake said, staring at the small cracks in the wood on the table. Abby didn't reply. She moved around the kitchen in silence, allowing him room to think and speak as she found mugs and fussed with the coffeemaker.

"I would like for you to return to Cherry Tree with me. I have had a lot of time to think lately, and I can't deny I have feelings for you. I want us...I was hoping we could," he began trailing and stumbling over his words. He knew what he wanted to say but didn't want to risk upsetting or offending her more.

"Jake, I don't want to get caught up in the middle of anything so complicated, I understand you have been through a lot lately, so I accept your apology. But...." she stopped, placing the mugs on the table between them. Jake waited for her to finish, but she didn't. His heart skipped a beat that there may be a possibility that she wanted him too.

He stood and came to stand alongside her, placing his hands gently on her shoulders, caressing her with his thumbs. She didn't look at him, which broke his heart a little. He knew he would have to work to earn her respect again. At the same time, she didn't move away. Was there hope?

"Please, will you give me a chance to make things right? Hear me out, and if you don't want to talk to me again, I will respect your wishes and leave you alone. But please let me try," he begged.

She finally looked up at him, sighing before gently pulling away. "I need time...but okay," she agreed.

Jake's grin was so wide that it nearly split his face. Suddenly, the world looked brighter. The heavy weight that had been upon his shoulders was gone. It was all he could do to keep from grabbing her and dancing around the room. Abby even let out a small chuckle at his excitement. He told her that he had rented a cabin nearby and when she was ready, all she had to do was call.

He allowed her to have her space for the rest of the day. Somehow, he managed to keep his mind busy with work at the small cabin in the other side of the bay.

Slowly, Abby came around. They spent the next few days doing everything Abby loved most. They hiked in Acadia National Park, browsed local stores for unique and fun finds, and searched local bookstores. All the while, they were slowly getting to know each other. They fell into each other's company with ease, like it was second nature to be together.

Abby

ABBY APPRECIATED Jake's efforts but was still a little wary. She didn't like wasting her time. She didn't like drama, and more importantly, she didn't want to get hurt again.

Jake was always the perfect gentlemen, but he still hadn't explained to her anything about what had happened or why he'd acted the way he did. She knew Jen was a sensitive subject, but if he was serious about making a go of things and serious about her, he needed to open up. Abby decided that if he wasn't willing to be honest with her and discuss things like adults, there was no point in moving forward.

They had spent the day enjoying the sun with their makeshift picnic lunches on a hike through the park again. They sat down to eat in a beautiful clearing where the sun danced off the trees. Abby took a breath and finally asked what she had wanted to ask since his arrival in Bar Harbor.

"Jake, what exactly happened? We haven't spoken about it much, and all I know is what I read in TMZ. If you are serious about seeing something here, between us, let's talk about this," Abby said with as much confidence as she could, trying to hide the way her hands trembled. She grabbed her water bottle to give her fingers something to do.

Jake finished eating the bite of his sandwich and took a sip of water to wash it down before he spoke. He reiterated everything he had told Abby previously about his past with Jen before processing his thoughts. "I was feeling the pull of the baby. A child is all I have ever wanted. Still, given everything with Silva, I wanted a paternity test," he began, watching Abby closely as she listened.

She nodded. She could understand this.

"Abby, when I saw the sonogram and heard the heartbeat, my life was decided at that moment. My future changed. I couldn't see anything but the baby. When we got outside, she said she wanted an abortion. I convinced her to take a paternity test first, and thankfully, she agreed." Jake took a moment, and she could tell her he was choosing his next words carefully.

"I guess a part of me thought I could convince her not to go ahead with the abortion. Maybe I could take the child and raise it. It's selfish, I know, but when the results came through, proving I wasn't the father and not only that, but she was keeping the baby to raise it with him...."

Jake's expression went blank, as though he'd been hollowed out, his gaze distant. Abby swallowed hard. She knew just how fresh and raw the memories were. She imagined he battled with himself not to feel anger.

"I felt like I'd been kicked in the stomach. Like the promise of happiness, all my hopes and dreams dangled in front of me, only to have someone rip them from me and laugh in my face," he said, running his hands through his hair.

Abby nodded. Tears pricked at the edges of her eyes.

"Up to that point, before I found out the baby wasn't mine, whenever anything happened, all I wanted to do was call you, to talk to you. I couldn't stop thinking about you and how all my drama must have made you feel. But then, when Silva and Jen said they were raising the baby, all I felt was pain and rejection, and there you were, representing happiness and joy."

Abby sat staring at him. She didn't know how to process what he said, but she knew he wasn't finished and needed to get this out. His shoulders had tensed when she had asked him her question. But the more he talked, the more she saw him visibly uncoil and relax. Slowly, she leaned closer and rested her hand on his, silently telling him to continue.

"I got drunk and angry and wasn't thinking straight. I felt like I had failed. There must have been something I had done wrong to make Jen want to get rid of the baby if it was mine but keep it with Silva. I hated myself. I wanted to feel the pain and the hurt, and you made me think of anything and everything good in my life. I snapped at you and aimed my anger at the one person who was there for me the most." He blinked back tears.

She nodded, trying not to cry herself.

He grabbed Abby's hand and turned to her, staring deeply and lovingly into her eyes. "I can't tell you how sorry I am," he said simply.

Looking into his eyes and seeing the lines on his face, she knew he was a good man, and he meant what he said. Without saying a word, she pulled him into her embrace, and they sat wrapped in each other's arms. They didn't need to say anything. The hug said it all.

Not wanting to pull back or let him go, but knowing she had to, Abby was the one to finally step back. She turned toward Jake. "I can't deny there is something here with us. I don't know what it is, but I am willing to try and find out. But I don't do drama, and I'm getting too old to be wasting my time. This is your first and only chance." She smiled, lifting one hand to touch his cheek lightly. "Who knows? As the kids say, we might end up being besties, but I'm willing if you are to see what might be there."

Jake was ecstatic, and Abby couldn't help but laugh at how much like a kid he looked with that wide grin. He was still a gentleman and insisted they do things right. They arranged to have their first official date the following night. Abby wanted to know the plan. She wasn't a big fan of surprises, especially where first dates were concerned. However, she trusted Jake, so in the end, she agreed he could set things up the way he wanted without telling her first. Maybe not all surprises were bad.

Abby

ABBY FELT LIKE A TEENAGER AGAIN. It had been the longest time since she had been on a first date and even longer since she had been so nervous and excited about going out at all. She tried to probe Jake for hints about what they were doing, mostly because she didn't know what to wear.

Jake attempted flattery and insisted she could wear her PJs and would still look amazing. Eventually, he told her to dress for dinner, but that was as much information as she would get. Abby hadn't packed anything suitable for a fancy dinner when she first traveled to Cherry Tree Island, so she decided a day of shopping might calm her nerves and soothe the butterflies that ran wild in her stomach. After perusing several shops, she settled on a simple yet elegant black calf-length pencil skirt and a white silk blouse with a black and gold belt. She even treated herself to a new pair of high heels.

As she readied herself for the night, she tied her hair up in a high ponytail and curled the ends, putting the last touches of her makeup on; she heard the knock on the door. She looked herself over in the mirror before opening the door. Her eyes lit up when she saw him, even as her stomach did somersaults. Jake looked so dashing and handsome.

He stood holding yet another bouquet. His simple black suit with a white shirt gave him a touch of elegance. She liked how he had left it an open collar, and she could make out a small patch of chest hair, just curling over the edges of the fabric in a sexy yet tantalizing way.

She chuckled. "If you keep buying me flowers, I will run out of places to put them." Feeling brave, she took the flowers from him and leaned in to kiss him on the cheek gently. He wore a cologne that made her think of wood smoke and spice, making Abby's cheeks blush beet red as her mind raced. As she stood back, she repressed a laugh at the look on Jake's face. He reminded her of a boy who had just been kissed for the first time. Once the shock wore off, a smile spread across his face, lighting his eyes up in the process.

"Abby, wow, you look so beautiful," he said as he followed her inside.

"Thank you. You look very handsome yourself." She hummed a happy tune half under her breath as she hunted down a vase to place her flowers. "So, where are we headed tonight?" she asked after they were arranged. She grabbed her small velvet clutch bag on the counter, ready to go.

"It's a surprise," he winked.

She laughed. "Haven't we established that already?"

Jake took her hand and brought it to his lips, gently pressing a kiss across her knuckles. Heat spread through her, and she blushed at his touch.

"Shall we go?" he asked. Abby nodded, and they left the cabin hand in hand.

Jake had a town car waiting for them. As they drove toward the Harbor, Abby looked out of the window to determine what Jake could have planned.

The sun had begun to set, and the view over the water was breathtaking. It filled Abby with a sense of romance, and she drew in a sharp breath of anticipation, excited at what the evening might hold.

Abby let out a little gasp as the car pulled up at the harbor. An impressive private yacht was moored at the dock, waiting for them to board. The name Sunset Love was scrolled in beautiful calligraphy on the side. It wasn't an overly grand yacht, but it was still pretty impressive. It had several decks and had been decorated with strings of lights and large vases full of roses and lilies.

"Welcome to our first date," Jake said with a smile, taking Abby's hands and leading the way down to the dock. The closer Abby got to the yacht, the more extravagant it seemed. She knew Jake was a successful businessman, but she didn't think he had enough cash to afford something like that. Her gut twisted as she felt a little out of place. For the first time, worry crept into the back of her mind, a concern that she didn't fit or belong in his world.

"Jake is this your yacht?" she asked, still in awe as they approached the end of the marina and prepared to board.

Jake let out a small chuckle and glanced over at Abby with a smile. "No, I don't have much interest in these things. I borrowed it from a client. He is obsessed with yachting. This particular boat is actually the smallest he owns. I just wanted to do something special for this evening." He gestured for her to board ahead of him, following close behind.

Onboard, Abby gasped as she looked around. Mahogany and white enamel covered every surface. Abby was amazed at how every space was fitted so perfectly for comfort as they toured the boat. Large windows gave access to views, each more beautiful than the last. On one of the higher decks, they paused in a doorway which opened into an opulent dining room. Abby saw an elegantly made-up dining table, big enough for at least eight people. It looked like something out of a Hollywood movie. A simple single red rose sat in a clear crystal vase in the center of the table. Candles that smelled of vanilla and jasmine had been carefully placed around the room, filling it with a warm atmosphere that could wrap around you like a lover's embrace.

"Jake, this is beautiful," she breathed as he pulled out a chair for her to sit down.

"Not as beautiful as you," he said, his voice low and sexy.

"You're such a smooth talker," she teased, patting him gently with her clutch bag.

Jake sat next to her at the large round table, draped in a bright white silk tablecloth. Abby had been so captivated by the yacht's beauty that she hadn't noticed the three young servers in the far corner. A tall young blonde wearing a black knee-length skirt and white blouse with a black tie stepped forward.

"Would you prefer red or white wine this evening?" she asked with a smile and a slight bow.

"Red, please," Abby answered, and the young woman nodded gracefully and turned, heading down a small set of stairs. Jake glanced over and laughed a little at the confusion plastered on Abby's face.

"What's wrong?" he asked with a smile.

"Oh nothing, I just didn't expect to have servers," she said.

"Yeah, Mike loves to be over the top. When I asked if I could borrow the Sunset Love, he insisted I use a few of his staff to help this evening," Jake answered, rubbing the back of his neck in a gesture she found endearing.

"Nervous?" Abby teased with a wink.

"You make me nervous. You also make me smile," he answered smoothly.

Abby had to force herself not to roll her eyes. She liked Jake, but so far on this date that hadn't even really begun, she felt like she was seeing a pretentious, almost fake poser side to him that she didn't like. The young woman returned with a bottle of wine and poured them both a glass before excusing herself. Another brought over a menu, and after they had picked their starter, main, and dessert, she too left them in peace. After a glass of wine, Abby relaxed a little. She decided she was just nervous and probably over-reacting to everything. Jake was a great guy.

Over dinner, they spoke a little more about the situation with Jen and how Jake now just wished them the best. He told her about his friend Trent and his family and gave her an insight into what he did for a living. Abby told him how far she was getting along with her novel and talked about what her kids had been up to lately. After a while, the conversation shifted to their childhoods, music, movies, and everything else you discuss on a first date. It was shaping up to be a lovely evening.

After dinner had been cleared, the young blonde server brought out a bottle of champagne. Abby wouldn't usually mix her drinks but felt rude refusing. Jake led her up to the top deck, where they could view the night sky. It was beautiful. The sky was shades of dark blue, twinkling with stars, and the moon's reflection danced on the water.

"Can I have this dance?" Jake asked, holding out his hand.

"There is no music," Abby laughed. The third young woman who had silently followed them now pulled out a violin and began playing as if on cue. Taken by the moment, Abby mock curtsied and took Jake's hand.

She loved how it felt to be in his strong arms. She rested her head on his shoulder, inhaling his masculine scent. She closed her eyes and let him lead as they danced slowly along with the music. It was her movie moment, and she didn't want it to end.

"I have another surprise," Jake whispered in her ear after their second? Third? Dance. Abby had lost count; she was simply enjoying the moment. Jake pointed across the water to the other side of the harbor. The next minute, the sky lit up in green, pink, purple, and blue shades as fireworks danced across the night sky.

While Abby craned her neck and admired the beautiful shapes and colors flashing in front of her eyes, that same uncomfortable feeling she had earlier started creeping back in. Was this how he acted on all his first dates? While it was nice, Abby could see how the special treatment would work on a girl like Jen or even one of the girls serving them. Abby liked things simple. All of this extravagance unsettled her. The final straw was when Jake sat her down and presented her with his gift, a diamond and sapphire tennis bracelet. While it was a stunning piece of jewelry, it was far too much for Abby. She gracefully took the bracelet and set it down beside her. She took Jake's hands and gave them a gentle squeeze with a sigh. He looked back at her with big puppy dog eyes.

She sighed. This wasn't going to be easy.

"Jake, while this has been a lovely, truly magical evening, I think it's time for me to go home. And thank you so much for the gift, but I can't accept it," she said, stroking her thumb over his skin, trying her best to let him down gently.

"Have I done something wrong?" he asked, worry creasing his eyes.

"No, not at all. It's been a date I will never forget; it's just.... A bit much. Jake, I'm a simple woman. I don't need all this. I'd prefer to get to know you as we did before, on Cherry Tree," she said with a smile, picking the bracelet up and handing it back to him.

To her surprise, relief rushed over his face.

Jake

JAKE LET OUT a belly laugh and ran his hands over his face, roughing up his neatly combed hair.

"I guess I got carried away trying to impress you. I'm sorry. Mike convinced me the OTT stuff would work. I guess I am a little out of touch." He laughed and passed Abby the bracelet back. "I still want you to have this," he said, and his eyes told Abby he wasn't going to take no for an answer.

What could she do? She gave him a joking eye roll and presented her wrist. Jake placed it on her and fastened the clasp, allowing his fingers to stroke her wrist a little as he did before. Once again, he kissed her hand.

"I have an idea," he said, with a mischievous glint in his eyes.

"Shoot," Abby said with a smile, admiring the bracelet that fit her wrist perfectly. Maybe some of these over-the-top things were okay. Sometimes.

"Come back to Cherry Tree with me. Let's turn back the clock from before tonight to before Jen and the baby. Back to the last place where everything was great: the night of the storm. Well, without you being sick, of course," he said, staring at Abby, hoping she would agree.

She took a sip of her champagne and tossed the idea around in her head for a minute. And she took another sip of her drink. Jake knew she was teasing him, making him wait as he had with her, but it was agonizing. He began to bounce his knee nervously before she turned to him and smiled.

"When do we leave?" she asked with a wink.

Jake scooped her up into his arms and spun them both around. Abby let her head fall back and giggled, dizzy from the spinning and all the indulgence of the evening. When Jake stopped, he looked down at her and gently brought his lips down to hers. His heart fluttered as she kissed him back. He tasted like chocolate, strawberries, and champagne.

As the moon rose higher in the sky and the date ended, Jake took Abby back to her cabin. They lingered at the front door. This time, she kissed him. He ran his fingers up the back of her neck, stroking her jaw with his thumb. She hummed her enjoyment against his lips before excusing herself and wishing him a good night's sleep.

Back at his cabin, sleep eluded Jake. He was too replete with energy and excitement. He could still feel her lips on his and smell her Chanel perfume. He chuckled to himself. "I'm like a lovesick teenager."

Jake and Abby sank back into island life when they got home. It was like nothing had happened. It felt so natural and right, like they had always been meant to live on their isolated island together. Together, they enjoyed a simple life.

Jake, being a gentleman, insisted he stay in the Annex. He didn't want to rush Abby or presume anything. She appreciated the gesture, and it put her at ease. But as weeks turned to months, she found herself going to bed frustrated and longing for him. She wanted him close, to hold her and kiss her. She respected his decision that if anything were ever to happen, it would be on her terms when she was ready. But that didn't stop her mind from wandering. She found she was nervous about being so vulnerable around Jake, about opening herself up to him, even though she trusted him completely.

Didn't she?

They spent their time enjoying the island, helping Bobbi – much to Bobbi's insistence that she could manage things alone. They cooked a new recipe every night. Some evenings they played board games. They watched a host of movies. Some evenings they did nothing at all, sitting in each other's arms just reading, either a book each or out loud to each other. They even spent some time traveling and exploring nearby restaurants and shops.

Abby found she didn't like sleeping alone anymore at the end of the third month. Her thoughts of Jake had kept her company for as long as possible. She poured herself a cup of coffee and headed to the widow's walk. Looking out over the beauty she had come to call home, she finally knew contentment, with a smile on her face and warmth in her heart. She spied Jake swimming, the sun dancing off his muscular shoulders. Her heart beat faster, and her grip tightened around her cup.

Jake was truly glorious. When he stepped out of the water, his body glistened in the sun. Her mind wandered. That was that. She'd made her decision. Tonight, Jake would share her bed.

Jake had spent the rest of the day in the Annex catching up on some work. Abby was well aware of how much he had neglected his work as of late, and she didn't want to distract him any more than she already had. Abby decided she also needed to make more progress with her novel. She had enjoyed writing it so far but lately had been neglecting it as she indulged in her new peaceful way of life.

She had finished half her manuscript by four o'clock and sat back satisfied. The ideas flowed through her fingers like magic. Cherry Tree inspired her more than she could have imagined. Her blood raced with excitement and energy. She was happier than she could ever remember. She went upstairs to shower and dressed in a simple yet sexy black dress she had bought on their last shopping trip. She fixed her hair and applied a minimal amount of makeup to heighten her features yet still look natural. Then, she started dinner.

Jake knocked on the door just after seven. His jaw dropped as his eyes caught sight of her at the door.

"Wow, Abby, you.... wow," he said, making Abby blush and the hairs on the back of her neck stand on end, sending an electric shiver down her spine.

They ate dinner and drank wine while talking about Jake's work, which Abby understood a lot better now than when she first arrived on the island. She told him about the progress she was making on her novel and thought of an inventive twist to keep the readers guessing. Jake tried to probe her for more information, but she chuckled, enjoying teasing him.

"You will just have to buy a copy and read it to find out."

Before they knew it, they had finished two bottles of wine, and they sat wrapped in each other's arms on the sofa watching a rom-com on Netflix. The wine gave Abby an extra nudge of courage as she watched the lovers on the screen embrace and caress one another. Her skin prickled, imagining how it would feel to have Jake touch her like that. Before she could talk herself out of it, she turned her head and pulled Jake to her, bringing his lips to hers in a deep passionate kiss that left them both light-headed. One kiss led to another. Not wanting the moment to end or to lose her nerve, she took Jake by the hand and led him upstairs. They made love until sleep wrapped around them, and the moon shone high in the sky above.

"Morning, beautiful," Jake said softly, kissing Abby on the forehead as her eyes fluttered awake.

"Morning back," she smiled, snuggling deeper into Jake's arms, resting her head on his chest. "I like waking up in your arms," she said before she could stop herself.

Jake kissed her on the forehead once again and stroked her shoulder tenderly. "I like waking up with you in my arms," he replied.

A week later, work called. Jake couldn't avoid it much longer. He kissed Abby and told her he would be back as soon as possible. Neither wanted to be apart for too long. As he headed back to Portland, Abby sank back into her writing, filled with new ideas, inspiration, and a new lust for life....and for Jake.

Jake

JAKE HAD SPENT the last two weeks in Portland. Two weeks too long, as far as he was concerned. He missed Cherry Tree and his new life, but most of all, he missed Abby.

While in Portland, Jake had dropped by to visit Trent and the family. Trent seemed to have some idea of what was going on after seeing his friend so happy. He told Jake he looked happier than he had seen him in as long as he could remember.

"I want to meet this mystery woman," Trent said, nudging Rosie for moral support.

"That sounds great. We could use a break. Perhaps we could pop over to Cherry Tree for the weekend," she winked back at Trent as she cleared the dinner table.

"Can we? Can we really? Oh please, Uncle Jake, can we come?" Max asked, excitement drumming in him as he bounced around the table, tugging at Jake's sleeve.

Jake laughed and picked up the small boy sitting in his lap. "Sure, why not?" he smiled as Max cheered and swung his arms around Jake's neck, squeezing so tight Jake joked that he was as strong as The Hulk. Delighted by the outing, he texted Abby to give her a heads up.

'On my way back. I have a surprise. See you soon. Jake xxx'

Happy with his text, he hit send. It didn't take long for Abby to reply with a series of cheerful-looking emoticons. He smiled at his phone and shoved it back in his pocket.

"She must be something special. Look at that grin on your face," Rosie teased, poking Jake in the shoulder.

Jake smiled back. "She is, she truly is."

As they arrived back at the island, the first thing Jake saw was Abby standing at the end of the dock, waving, anticipating their arrival. Rosie gave Jake another playful jab in the arm as the boat sailed closer.

"She's beautiful, Jake. No wonder you're acting like a young buck again!" she chuckled.

Abby welcomed them all with open arms upon their arrival, lifting Max into the air as he cheered.

"I like her, mommy," the young boy said, suddenly getting shy and hiding behind Rosie, making everyone laugh.

"I thought it was about time you met my closest and oldest friend, Trent, his wife Rosie, and their son Max. Max, meet Abby," Jake said, wrapping his arm around Abby and pulling her close during the introductions, kissing her on the head when he finished speaking.

"I've heard so much about you all. It's so lovely to meet you. I wish Jake had told me we were expecting guests. I would have made more effort." Abby laughed, looking down at her denim shorts and a plain white t-shirt.

"Oh nonsense, you look fabulous," Rosie said, linking Abby's arm through hers and heading up to the main house.

The weekend went by in a blur of laughter, fun, and newfound friendships. Abby felt like she had found a good friend in Rosie. They talked as though they'd known each other forever. Max adored Abby and clung to her side whenever possible. Abby probed Trent for juicy stories about Jake, and she told him all about herself and her kids. Their friendship was as natural to her as her relationship with Jake had proven to be.

The more Jake watched his friends accept Abby as one of their own, the more he was sure Abby was the right person for him.

Sunday flew around way too quickly, and Max protested going

home, begging to stay longer. Still, Rosie and Trent insisted it was time their visit came to an end.

"Don't worry, sweetie, you can come to visit anytime," Abby said, hugging him close.

Max didn't want to let her go. "Promise?" he asked.

"Of course. And Abby and Jake can come to visit us anytime," Trent said, winking at Abby.

"Don't be saying your goodbyes yet. We're not leaving until after dinner. It's barely noon, and I still have a bit of sunbathing to do," Rosie said with a chuckle.

Abby and Rosie bathed in the sun while watching Max play in the sand. Trent and Jake went inside to check on the baby. Bobbi had insisted on babysitting and was a natural. She hardly saw her niece, so she was more than happy for any chance to look after a baby.

Trent and Jake sat in the shade outside the main house, happy to get a little bro-alone time.

"Man, I can't remember the last time I saw you this happy. I swear you have a glow about you." Trent cracked a beer and took a sip. "And... yep, defiantly a few more wrinkles around the eyes from all the smiling," he teased.

"What can I say? Abby is a wonderful woman," Jake said, his heart filling with joy and warmth and his stomach filling with butterflies at her name. "I love her, Trent, no two ways about it. I'm head over heels, sickeningly, hopelessly in love with her. She holds my heart in her hands." It felt so good and so right to say it out loud. It made his feelings real. He wanted to shout his love from the rooftops.

"Have you told her?" Trent asked.

Jake shook his head. He sat back, let his head fall back, and laughed. "Who would have thought it, me, my age. Acting like a kid just finding his first love," Jake joked.

"Does she feel the same?" Trent asked.

"God, I hope so." Jake breathed out a short breath, his heart aching at the thought of her not reciprocating his feelings.

"You have to tell her," Trent said, patting his friend on the back. "I can tell. You two are the real deal. Goals, as the kids say these days." The two old friends looked at each other before falling into roars of laughter.

Abby

~~~~

THE FOLLOWING DAY, Abby woke to the smell of bacon, eggs, toast, and coffee. She stretched and rubbed her eyes, sitting up as Jake walked into the room carrying a tray piled high with food.

"I thought we might have breakfast in bed this morning." He set the tray down carefully and cuddled up next to Abby. A warmth spread over her as she was filled with happiness, contentment, and gratitude for everything she had. She often thought, lately, about how lucky she was. She leaned across and kissed Jake gently on the lips. He tasted of toothpaste and the scent of his shower gel that reminded her of the cologne he wore on their "first date" on the yacht. She picked up her coffee, inhaling the dark roast before taking a sip.

"Trent and Rosie are lovely. They make such an adorable little family," Abby said.

Jake smiled. His joy radiated off him like the summer sun that shone through the window. "They are like my family. I love them dearly. I'm so glad you all got along. I think you have a new fan. Max couldn't get enough of you." He laughed and took a bite of toast.

Abby chuckled, "I think he stole my heart," she said, holding her hand to her chest.

"I hope not. That's mine to steal," Jake joked.

Abby looked over to him and noticed his shoulders had tensed, and a look of apprehension filled his eyes.

"What's wrong?" she asked, suddenly worried. They hadn't talked about children. She knew she didn't want anymore, but kids still held a part of Jake's heart.

She didn't understand why they hadn't had the conversation yet, perhaps the two of them were not ready to talk about it, or maybe Jake still found children a sore subject. But while she looked up at him waiting, she braced herself for an awkward conversation. What would she say if he asked about kids in their future? Was she open to thinking about it? Was adoption an option? She didn't know.

"I...I...there is," Jake stumbled.

Abby placed her hand on his knee, letting him know she was there, whatever he needed to say. "There is something I have wanted to tell you for a while, and after talking to Trent, I realized I should have said it a long time ago," he continued.

Abby felt her shoulders tighten but tried to hide it, smiling slightly up at him. "Okaaaay," she said cautiously.

"I love you, Abby." He couldn't quite meet her gaze, like a scared child.

Relief surged through her. "I love you too," she said, her face lighting up like a beautiful spring morning. Jake cupped her cheek before placing a soft, gentle kiss on her lips. It was a kiss that, even in its gentleness, spoke of the love they both shared.

They ate breakfast, chatted about the weekend, laughed, and talked about how Abby had replaced Jake as Max's favorite person. After a while, Abby felt a wave of sadness and longing wash over her. She sighed deeply and placed her empty cup back on the tray.

"What's wrong?" Jake asked.

"Oh, nothing... it's just that while this weekend and the past few months have been.... more amazing than words can say, I miss my kids. I haven't spoken to them properly in the longest time. I'm afraid I have forgotten the sound of their voices," Abby said, trying to make a joke of the last part, but her pain was real no matter how she tried to hide it.

As the days passed, Abby found herself longing for her kids more and more, but every time she picked up her phone to call, she couldn't. She felt a guilt stab at her that she hadn't tried to reach out sooner, that she had been so wrapped up in her new love and the island that she'd pushed them right out of her mind.

One morning, she stood on the widow's walk, looking out over the view, pulling her cardigan a little tighter around her. The sun shone brightly, but there was a cold breeze in the air, telling Abby that the weather was due to change soon. She didn't mind. She actually thought a little rain might be nice. It had been oddly hot lately, and rain might clear the air.

She watched as a boat pulled closer to the dock. As it got closer, she noticed Jake at the wheel. She hadn't realized he had left the island. She loved watching him behind the boat wheel; he looked so strong and rugged. Suddenly, her eye was drawn to two people tucked in the back, trying to hide out of sight. When the boat stopped and Jake stepped onto the dock, Abby's heart skipped a beat as Jake turned to help Kim out of the boat. Kyle closely followed behind. She almost dropped her coffee.

She ran down the stairs, taking them two at a time, and raced to the dock.

"Mom," Kim yelled, hurtling toward her. Kim waved her hands high and jumped excitedly. Abby almost knocked Kim over when they ran into each other's arms, wrapping her up tightly, not wanting ever to let her go again.

"What about me? I'm here too." Kyle chuckled and stepped forward for a hug.

"I can't believe you are here." Abby breathed the words in his ear. She inhaled both of them, remembering how they smelled. How could she have forgotten? Beautiful memories flooded her mind and her eyes brimmed with tears of joy.

"I have missed you both so much. I can't even tell you. Let me look at you." Abby said, stepping back and soaking up her children.

"I contacted them the other day. I thought it would be a nice surprise for you," Jake said from behind them.

Abby practically jumped into his arms. Kim and Kyle groaned

mockingly, complaining about "old people and public displays of affection."

"Wow. Mom normally hates surprises. You must be something special," Kim said, smiling.

"Yeah, that or...." Kim jabbed him in the ribs with her elbow cutting her brother off before he said something embarrassing. Jake and Abby laughed with them as they helped them with their bags.

How long had it been since Abby saw her kids? It couldn't have been too long, could it? Abby didn't know or care. She was just happy to see them. They seemed to have grown so much in the short time since she'd seen them last. The subtle changes of their growing maturity had her heart filled, bursting with pride.

"So, Mom, can we get a tour?" Kim asked after they had put their bags in the Annex.

Abby took her hand, and Kyle and Jake followed behind as they walked around the island. Abby couldn't remember a time she was happier. She had a great guy living on a beautiful island, was finally taking steps toward her dream of writing, and now her kids were here.

What more could I ask for?

At dinner, Kim and Kyle talked about how school was going. Kim couldn't stop talking about all her new friends, and Kyle was very proud of his new part-time job. Abby smiled and laughed so much that her face hurt. Her heart ached, but not with longing or pain. It ached with unconditional love, the kind of love only a mother could feel.

"I love you all so much. This has been the greatest surprise ever," Abby said as tears of joy brimmed in her eyes. She found she was welling up with tears of happiness a lot lately. She often lay in bed thanking the heavens for everything she had in her life to be grateful for.

Jake took Kyle out on the boat after he insisted that he wanted to learn to drive it, leaving the girls on the island to catch some sun and have a swim.

"I'm really happy for you, Mom. I can't remember ever seeing you like this. You are glowing and not just from the sun. You radiate happiness. It's a joy to be around," Kim said as she poured herself some more lemonade.

The care and love in her daughter's voice meant the world to Abby.

"Thank you, sweetie; I really am the happiest I've ever been," Abby said, accepting her drink and adjusting her sunglasses.

"Jake is great. I approve! I'm pretty sure Kyle only insisted on going out on the boat so he could give him the *if you hurt my mom...* talk," Kim said, sending them both into fits of laughter.

The thought of her son protecting her like that filled her with such pride, even if she could imagine Jake trying to control his laughter in the process.

"He brings out the best in me," Abby began, her heart racing at the thought of her novel and finally sharing it with her daughter. "Did I ever tell you I once dreamed of writing?" she asked, knowing full well she hadn't.

Kim shook her head and looked at Abby with a twinkle in her eyes. "To be honest, Mom, I never knew you had dreams. You dedicated all your life to Kyle and me. I used to worry you had lost yourself and didn't know what made you happy anymore," Kim said.

Abby reached over and hugged her daughter tightly. "You and Kyle were my dream, darling. Being your mother brought me joy and happiness I could never put into words." She beamed, holding Kim's face in both hands and just looking at her offspring, admiring the woman her daughter had become.

"As I was saying, I mentioned it to Jake, and one thing led to another, and...well, I have just finished it," Abby said with a slight blush. She didn't know why she was embarrassed but couldn't help feeling it anyway. Maybe it was nerves over sharing her dream with someone else, especially with someone who mattered so much to her.

Kim jumped to her feet with excitement, almost knocking over their drinks. She grabbed her mom's hand and pulled her toward the main house. "You have to show me; please, Mom, please!"

With a chuckle at her daughter's enthusiasm, Abby followed. Once inside, she sat biting her nails with nerves as Kim read.

"It's just for fun, but I enjoyed it," Abby said dismissively, trying to take the laptop out of her daughter's grip after a few minutes, thinking her daughter had probably had enough. Only Kim wouldn't let the computer go. She was enthralled, not wanting to stop reading.

"Mom, this is amazing. Who is the killer? No, don't tell me. I want to find out myself. Oh, when you sell this to a big publisher, can I have your first autographed copy?" Kim asked with all seriousness.

"Oh, those big publishers wouldn't be interested in me. It's just a fun project that I had wanted to toy around with, nothing more," Abby insisted, leading them back out to enjoy the rest of the afternoon sun before they started dinner.

Jake

~⌒⌒⌒

"YOU'RE BACK. That means Kyle didn't crash," Kim teased her brother as Jake and Kyle joined them just in time for dinner.

"He's a natural," Jake said, and the pair shared a fist bump, which made the girls laugh harder than they expected.

"Dinner will be ready soon. Kyle, would you care to help me?" Abby asked as she began setting the table.

"Jake, can I borrow you for a second?" Kim asked.

Jake held his hands up in surrender. "Oh no, is this another, *don't hurt my mom* talk?" Jake teased as Kyle shot him a jokingly angry glare.

Abby and Kim erupted into laughter.

"I told you," Kim said to Abby before taking Jake's arm and leading him out of the room. Once out of earshot, Kim presented Jake with her mom's laptop. She explained her conversation with Abby and asked for his help.

"I knew she was writing. I didn't know she had finished. I will do everything I can to help her dream come true, I promise," Jake said.

That seemed to be enough for Kim, who smiled and flung her arms around him. "I've never seen Mom so happy. You are good for her. But if you hurt her, Kyle will be the least of your worries," she said, jabbing him in the arm.

It didn't hurt, but Jake played it off like it did, rubbing his arm before saluting Kim. "Affirmative; orders heard loud and clear," he said with a wink, and they headed back in for dinner.

Abby was sad to see her kids leave, but she didn't want them to miss any more of their schoolwork. She had so enjoyed their company. Finally, alone for what felt like the first time in ages, she thanked Jake properly for such a wonderful surprise.

The following morning Jake rose before Abby. When she woke up, he was dressed and packed a small bag. Abby looked at him in alarm.

"Nothing to worry about, just an urgent call from the office. I need to head back to Portland for a few days. I'll be back as soon as possible," he said, kissing her deeply before speeding off.

He had another surprise up his sleeve for Abby and was filled with excitement and adrenaline. He didn't want to wait to make it happen.

Abbu

ABBY SAT up bewildered at how quickly and eagerly Jake had left. Something in her mind told her he was lying. He wasn't just going to Portland to work; he had packed a small bag. Usually, he didn't pack anything when he went to Portland for work. What did he need to pack? He had a house in Portland. Abby strolled up to the widow's walk and watched the boat sail toward the mainland. Her mind raced.

"You are being silly, Abby," she said as if saying the words out loud would make her calm and think rationally.

She showered, dressed, and headed down for food. The house, and even the island, were so quiet. After the sudden rush of visitors, Abby had forgotten how peaceful the island could be. She had grown accustomed to having people around her, and now Jake had sped away. She felt a pang of loneliness that she couldn't explain.

After breakfast, she decided to browse the internet for news on the outside world. Her laptop was sitting waiting for her open on the coffee table in the living room. *Odd, I don't remember leaving it there,* she thought, then shrugged the thought away. The previous days had been a little hectic. It was easy for her to forget where she left things.

It wasn't cold, but Abby still found comfort in wrapping a blanket around herself as she sipped her coffee and scanned through the local news and gossip sites. Nothing too exciting, just the same old stories on politics, a few scientific articles warning of the dangers of global warming, and a few celebrity scandals.

Wait.

That's when she saw it. Her heart almost stopped. She almost missed the table when she set her cup down, spilling coffee over her hand. She pulled the laptop into her lap to read the TMZ headline.

It was an article about Jen and Silva. They had split up. The accompanying picture showed Jen heavily pregnant. The report had been posted only fifteen minutes before Jake left. Was it a coincidence? She had no clue. She set the laptop down and headed to the kitchen to clean up, hoping that keeping her hands busy would stop her mind from spiraling and clean away the doubts.

What if seeing me with my kids made Jake realize how much he does want a baby? What if he saw the article and has sped off to see her? Would he want to raise someone else's baby with her? As if it were his own? They have a history. Why not? Her mind raced. Doubt stabbed at her mind giving her a headache.

Her heart felt like it could break. What would she do if he chose to go back to Jen? She couldn't remember being so happy, she never intended to fall for Jake, but she had. And she had fallen hard. Tears filled her eyes before she straightened up and slammed her hands on the counter.

"Enough!" she yelled to the empty sink. "No more acting like a child! You are a grown woman. Deal with what you must when you have to. Jake is a good man. He wouldn't hurt me like that!"

Or would he? She can give him something I can't. I don't want any more children. Damn, I knew we should have discussed this.

She pulled on her hiking boots and headed to Bobbi's cabin, pulling herself together. She knocked on the door and, thankfully, didn't wait too long before she answered.

"Hi Abby, is everything okay?" Bobbi asked with a smile, moving aside to let Abby inside.

"Everything is fine. I wondered if you needed any help today. I've been so busy lately with everyone coming to visit. I'm a little lost for something to do." She smiled, hoping Bobbi believed her lie. She knew she could talk to Bobbi; they had become good friends. But she didn't want to discuss what she was thinking if Bobbi confirmed her worries.

Bobbi smiled, seeming glad for the offer. "Sure, I was just making a to-do list for the day."

They spent the day tending to the gardens and harvesting what vegetables they could. Bobbi even convinced Abby to fish with her. Being so hands-on with Bobbi made Abby love the island more. She thought she knew this place like the back of her hand, but today it felt as though she was discovering something new every second. When they finally stopped and sat enjoying a cold drink together, Abby was filled with joy once more. Cherry Tree was home.

That feeling was confirmed when Jake arrived home the following day.

Jake

JAKE KNEW Abby didn't particularly like surprises. All the same, he had given her several over their time together, and she seemed to be coming around to them. She had loved everything he had done so far, but his next surprise would be his most significant. A cocktail of nerves and excitement had his stomach feeling like he had been on a roller coaster all day. But he loved it. He adored Abby and wanted nothing more than to see her smile.

He woke her to breakfast in bed. A single red rose with an envelope rested against the vase was on the tray.

"Morning, beautiful," he said softly as he rested the tray on the table closest to the bed and kissed her softly on the lips, smoothing hair out of her eyes as she woke.

She smirked. "Morning to you too, handsome. Breakfast in bed again? What do you have planned now?"

"Damn, do I have a tell? I guess I shouldn't play poker with you," he joked.

Abby picked up the envelope and pulled out a card detailing her day ahead. The fancy script read, "Abby's birthday celebration."

"What is this?" she asked with a smile.

"I'm sending you to Deer Isle for the night. I have a work project that I can't keep putting off, so I won't be able to join you. But don't worry, I will celebrate your birthday properly when you get back." He grinned.

"What's in Deer Isle?" she asked, one eyebrow rising as she glanced curiously at the invitation.

"A Spa Day. Bobbi will take you back to the mainland and drive you to the spa. Tomorrow, she will pick you up and bring you back," Jake said.

Abby gave him a look of suspicion. "What are you up to?"

He winked. "Go enjoy the spa. Relax, get a massage or whatever you ladies do, and you will find out the rest of your surprise tomorrow."

Jake spent the rest of the day making calls, arranging cars, and hoping he could get everything done on time. He had planned Abby's surprise down to the tiniest detail.

"Just like you said, she quizzed me all the way to the spa, asking what I knew," Bobbi said when she called to give him an update. Jake laughed. He wouldn't expect anything less.

"She's going to love it," Bobbi said, and Jake could hear her grin through the phone.

"I hope so," he said back, squeezing his hand around one of his two gifts for Abby, hoping she was right.

Abby

A KNOCK on the door made Abby jump. She didn't think she needed to or could be more relaxed than Cherry Tree had made her. But after a seaweed wrap, a mud mask, a hot oil hair treatment, and a full body massage, her muscles and joints felt like butter. *A girl could get used to this*, she thought cheekily. Opening the door, she was surprised to see a smartly dressed woman standing there, holding a garment bag in one hand and two bags, one medium and one small, in the other.

"Abby?" she asked, but Abby guessed she already knew the answer.

"Yes, can I help you?" Abby asked, pulling the fluffy belt of her robe tighter around her.

"These are from a Mr. Carver," she said with a beaming smile handing everything over to Abby.

A little taken back, Abby almost dropped everything.

"A Miss Roberta will be here to pick you up in an hour," the young lady said.

"Roberta? Oh, you mean Bobbi. Okay. Thank you and thank you for.... all this." Abby chuckled, shaking her head at the names of the stores on the sides of the bag. Jake was certainly sparing no expense. The young lady bowed and walked away.

Closing the door, Abby lay her gifts down on the bed. Opening the garment bag, she gasped. Inside was a beautiful off-the-shoulder red dress. Holding it up, Abby admired it. She didn't recognize the designer's name and thought the dress was a tad young for a woman her age. But once the silk touched her skin and she saw how the dress showed off her beautiful tan and toned shoulders, she forgot all that. She had never felt more beautiful. Inside one of the other bags was a pair of white Christian Louboutin heels and a matching white clutch. In the other, there was a simple pair of ruby earrings.

She stood looking at herself in the mirror, her hair curled and arranged in an elegant updo. She didn't want anything to distract from the beautiful dress, which quickly became her favorite. It hugged her waist and skimmed her knees. A simple touch of mascara and a bit of blush and lipstick was all she needed to be ready. She waited for Bobbi, her eyes still drawn to the reflection looking back at her. She heard Bobbi's rhythmic knock and opened the door. Bobbi wore a simple yet elegant black cocktail dress, her hair in a high ponytail. The pair gasped at each other's beauty.

"You look amazing," they said in unison, laughing.

"Come on. Your carriage awaits," Bobbi said, still chuckling.

"Please tell me he hasn't hired a carriage," Abby said in horror.

Bobbi erupted into giggles. "God, no. I'm driving us back to the marina, and then we take the boat as always," Bobbi answered.

As they approached the dock, Abby's eyes lit up. Cherry Tree had been decorated with lights and torches. A long dining table had been set up outside under the stars. And waiting in a simple black suit like on their first date was Jake, but he wasn't alone. Trent and Rosie stood by with Max. Next to them were Kim and Kyle and Abby's dear friend Marge. Everyone was dressed like movie stars and clapped, celebrating her arrival with Bobbi. A chorus erupted.

"Happy birthday, Abby!" they all said in unison, and Abby had to fight back the tears of happiness as her skin prickled with goosebumps at how beautiful it all was.

"I wanted to do something extra special for your birthday," Jake whispered in her ear as he pulled her into his embrace.

"I can't believe you are all here! This is so lovely. I can't thank you enough," Abby said, holding her hand to her chest.

"Don't thank us yet. The party hasn't even started," Marge said with a smile as she hugged Abby tightly. It had been so long since Abby had seen her dear friend that she forgot how much she missed her and made a mental note to visit her more often.

Jake had borrowed a few servers from his friend Mike's staff. Abby recognized two of the young ladies from the yacht. They served a beautiful dinner while a string quartet serenaded the guests. Kim and Kyle kept Max company, and everyone laughed when Max insisted on arguing with Kim and Kyle over who loved Abby more. Abby introduced Marge to everyone, and the friends chatted about everything they had missed from the past months. Abby didn't think the night could get any better.

As the night's air grew colder, Jake and Trent brought blankets outside for everyone to huddle under as they watched the firework display Jake had arranged.

"This is spectacular. I could never have wished for a better birthday," Abby gushed as she wrapped her arms around Jake. Kim snuck up beside them and playfully jabbed Jake in the side.

"Is it time? Is it time?" she asked. Excitement radiated off her, and her eyes sparkled like the stars. Jake nodded and pulled out an envelope.

"I can't take all the credit for this present. Kim gave me the idea," Jake said, pulling Kim into a hug as they all crowded around, waiting for Abby to read the letter.

Abby began to tremble, her hand shot to her mouth, and a stray tear slipped from her eye, splashing on the page as she read the words printed there.

"What is it?" Max asked.

"It's a letter from Mrs. Francis Underwood, the literary agent...." Abby began, reading the words over and over. She kept expecting to wake up. That it was all a dream, but as she felt Max tug on her skirt, she knew it wasn't. She scooped him up in her arms and carried on.

"She read my book and wants to represent me. She says she's confident she can get me a book deal. There is a list of five publishing houses that she has lined up for me," Abby finished, her voice catching in her throat.

"What book?" Kyle asked.

"Mom wrote a mystery novel. She showed it to me when we were here last, and I showed it to Jake," Kim chirped, pleased with herself.

"I took the novel to her last week, and she sent me that two days later," Jake said.

Abby looked up at him in awe. Tears flowed freely. She never thought her work would be good enough to publish, and the fact that two of the most important people in her life believed it was and had gone to such efforts for her, had left her overwhelmed. She didn't think her heart would hold any more love. Everyone cheered and hugged Abby in turn, congratulating her.

"Could this night get any better?" Abby joked, wiping her eyes. Everyone shared a look, and Abby rolled her eyes. Jake clearly had another surprise up his sleeve.

He stepped forward and took her hands in his. He placed a kiss softly on her head and took a deep breath before speaking. "We stood in the kitchen all those months ago while you prepared pasta for dinner. I asked you a question. Do you remember what it was?" he asked softly.

Abby could feel everyone around her buzzing with anticipation. Still, as she looked up into Jake's eyes, all she saw was him. She chuckled. "You asked me to marry you."

"And do you remember what you said?" He smiled.

Her heart began to race, her skin pricked with goosebumps, and the hair on the back of her neck stood on end. She laughed, suddenly aware of everyone waiting for her answer.

"I said if you keep chopping wood outside like that, I would." Everyone laughed with them. But the laughter stopped as Jake sank to one knee.

"If I promise to keep the wood box filled, would you make me the happiest man alive and be my wife?" he asked, opening a black velvet box showing a beautiful white gold cushion cut diamond ring.

The world stopped, all sound vanished, and all Abby could see was Jake kneeling in front of her with a ring. She was speechless. She wanted to scream yes, and leap into his arms, but she was paralyzed. Her head was dizzy with champagne bubbles and the joy from the evening.

"Come on, girl, don't keep the poor lad waiting. Think of his knees," Marge blurted out, making everyone laugh.

"Abby, will you marry me?" Jake asked again, a gentle plea in his voice.

This time, she couldn't stop the words from flying out. She couldn't stop herself from jumping into his arms and kissing him like they were the only two people on earth. "Yes! Yes! A million times, yes!" she cried as he slid the ring on her finger. It was a perfect fit.

Just like Abby and Jake. Just like Cherry Tree Island. Everything was absolutely perfect.

The End

Did you enjoy *Cherry Tree Island*?
Please consider rating it on Goodreads, Bookbub, or your favorite retailer.

Join my newsletter at www.daisylandishromance.com and never miss an update, a sale, or a giveaway!

About the Author

Daisy Landish is a clean romance and cozy mystery author whose clean and sweet novellas have tugged at readers' heartstrings around the world. When she's not writing love stories, Daisy spends her time reading, hiking at dawn, and riding into the sunset on her horse, Rosebud.

www.daisylandishromance.com

f facebook.com/daisylandishromance

X x.com/daisy_landish

instagram.com/daisylandishbooks

a amazon.com/author/daisylandish

BB bookbub.com/authors/daisy-landish

g goodreads.com/Daisy_Landish

Also by Daisy Landish

Clean Regency Romance

Christmas with the Earl

The Lady Series - The Allington Collection

The Lady Series - The Gillingham Collection

The Lady Series - The Blackmore Collection

The Lady Series - The Norrington Collection

Clean Contemporary Romance

Timeline Retreats - RomCom

Maplewood Grove Series - Small Town

Love on Spruce Island

Second Chance

Cherry Tree Island

The Wedding Trio

Extra Credit

Counting on the Cowboy

Focusing on the Cowboy

Mistletoe Magic

Grounded at Christmas

Cozy Mysteries

Lady Theodora Ashcombe Mysteries

Sophie Brooks Mysteries

Jane and Kennedy Daniels Mysteries

Pine Grove Mysteries

Annie Archer Paranormal Mysteries

Wilma Wade Holiday Mysteries

Mike and Maddie Mysteries

Mystic Moonhaven Mysteries

Sweater Weather: Cozy Mysteries for Fall

Summer Vibes: Cozy Mysteries for Summer

Let it Snow: Cozy Mysteries for Winter

Spring Break: Cozy Mysteries for Spring